Montana 3000

by
Sean Gallagher

For Lovey and Elliot: 2 angels I have met here.

Welcome, Reader!

Throughout human existence, our race has sought to answer the question 'why?' that surrounds so many of our common life experiences: war, love, death, soul, birth, time, et cetera. And to answer these questions, many civilizations have relied on allegory and myth to provide a framework for their epoch's attempt at explanation. So was it in antiquity, and so is it now in this, our very modern age.

The stories and their lessons that follow may seem equal parts discomforting and familiar to you. This is to be expected. The tales are discomforting because they trace the meanderings of a half-lived mind in crisis, a trajectory that is neither predictable nor placid.

Despite their strangeness, you're likely to find elements of these stories to be hauntingly resonant, as well. Again, this is to be expected. For while we like to remind ourselves of those things that make us unique, it is those things that make us the same that will ultimately save humanity.

But enough talk from me. I hope you enjoy exploring these stories and their lessons half as much as I enjoyed assembling them for your consideration. Happy reading!

Sean Gallagher
Writer, Montana 3000
10 February/Year 2023/F.N.A.

Montana 3000

morning is my favorite time

Morning is my favorite time. Before the sleepers shrug off their dreams; before they scrub the grit from their eyes and return to their roles. Before the world is roused back to its chaos. Breeze and birds accompany my reverie with subtle orchestration, and the sun's rising light brightens this, my thinking place. In the morning.

Most days I take my toast and tea on the loggia- in fact, I sit there now. From here I can see the whole thing unfold: the bees uncloistering to seek their pollen, the early-rising cogs rolling back to their wheels, the ants emerging from holes in search of heavy things to carry and new enemies to fight. Usually my newday thoughts self-steer and drift pleasantly about, bobbing and dipping- like a leaf, or a raft of dry moss riding the eddies of a gently swirling brook.

I try to think on things that bring me joy- sunrise is no time to dwell on undraped reality; there's plenty of time for that when the sun is high and the day longer-aged. Invariably, as happy thoughts ensue from this pleasant place, my brother floats in. My peace loving, my war-torn brother. Try as I might to confine my daydreams to his younger times, his salad days, I can't divorce what he was from what he has become. My beautiful, broken brother.

I remember once when we were kids, he defended me against a troop of punks. They were harassing me over some silly excuse. It was a lewd and unloved bunch. My brother stepped in, and I remember thinking, "Here comes the hammer, Jerks- prepare for your comeuppance." I knew he could take their three to his heroic one with a single stone fist- he was an invincible mountain to me. But rather than sweep clean the field, he took my hand and walked me away from battle, his back turned to the derision of those smaller souls. "What are you doing?!"

I cried. "We can take them, YOU can take them!" He just smiled. "No one wins a fight," was his self-possessed reply. I was scandalized and shamed by his cowardice.

Oft-confused was I by his unwillingness to wield his superior strength to advance a justified end. More than once I watched him smile down an aspirant foe, turning his squared and stone-hewn jaw away from the would-be defeated, as he was taught. As we're all taught, but seldom heed. How badly I wanted to watch him administer justice. To see him bloody his knuckles on the nose of the deserving and low-merited. I wanted to fight others with his fists- I yearned for vicarious violence, pleaded for it. But he was more monk than warrior- unrivaled in his power, unmatched in his disciplined restraint. I failed in my youthful ignorance to grasp his mastery and wisdom- I took it for weakness. On his behalf, I recklessly entreated those idols of veiled folly- the Gods of War- to uncloud his clouded eyes and embrace him into their fold. And Aries and Mars and Chiyou and Tohil and Odin and Anhur and god upon god, and all their minions, too- hearing my call- abided.

My brother received his Order to Arms on my 16th birthday. The war had been picking up speed and casualty numbers were increasing. There was wide speculation that another draft round was going to be needed, and sure enough, order messages started popping up across the Western Territories a few weeks before my brother got his.

It was a testament to the War Division's marketing acumen that things started off as popular as they did. No draft was needed for the first few years- lines wound around the block at the "Volunteer for Valor" kiosks planted near schools, travel ports, and food plazas throughout the Confederation and across the Protectorates. Boys and girls- in response to the government-issued goad- were eager to test their mettle, display their character, and earn their battle medallions, all while holding the moral high ground against a dead-eyed and hellbound rival. Coupled with the sempiternal gratitude of the Stay-At-Homes, and you had yourself a recipe for glory that many found difficult to resist. But as war scraped on and the supply of meat to the grinder slowed, new avenues of access into the body pool were needed, and that favored lever of Authority was eventually pulled: conscription.

To all the world, my brother embraced his call to duty and its noble gift therein ensconced: service to a greater good. But I was with him when he received his battle order, and I alone glimpsed the terror that flashed through him just before he regained the reins of his heroic composure. Here was a man conflicted: in love with peace and obliged to war.

As any younger brother or sister can attest, we consider it a sacred mandate of our set to- as near to always as possible- know the goings on of our older siblings. It was in exercise of this duty that I came to overhear a conversation between my brother and his sweetheart just prior to his departure for Combat Indoc. They were canoodled on a settee in the den and, to their false belief, alone. I was in the kitchen adjoining, taking advantage of some unique acoustics, the result of an air vent shared between the two rooms. My brother and his lover were engrossed in that timeless recreation enjoyed by all who approach the End of the Affair: the exchange of false promises.

Vows of immutable love were swapped, singularity of affection confirmed, and assurances of unfading feeling oathed- all of it sincere, and none of it true. But it was a soothing fiction for the Leaving and the Left Behind in this time of soon-parting. Once fidelity was pledged to the satisfaction of all parties, talk turned from love to an only-slightly less-serious topic: War Of Nations.

"Are you scared?" she queried. "Some," he confessed. "But nervous and excited, too....I'll get to see what's in me- what I'm capable of." "There are other ways, you know," she teased with a smiling voice. "Not when you're drafted," his mirthless reply. They continued to talk- and I to listen- for some time. Affirmations accompanied every rambling topic, and served to bolster the confidence and assuage the anxiety of the warrior-to-be: the cause was just, our force superior, victory close-at-hand, his quick return to her faithful arms imminent. Et cetera. Eventually, talk ascended to silence and the lovers returned to that country that lovers love most- the place of tender strokes and gentle moans. I took my leave at this, with my brother's words still ringing, "I'll get to see what's in me- what I'm capable of..."

He and I spoke only once after he posted to training garrison and before he saw battle. He was two weeks from completing Indoc, on a weekend pass, when he called me by VidLink from Battle Barracks Alpha: his temporary home at the war station in New Kingston- a place affectionately known by recruits as 'Killville.' My breath tripped when I saw him.

He was straddling that line- still, but just- between the familiar old and the unrecognizable and unreturnable new. He was stubble-headed and wore an armor of thick-corded muscle over his strapping frame. He was lean as a panther, and though his eyes hadn't yet fully transitioned into those of a predator, it was clear: the change was underway. He spoke with the confidence-bordering-brashness of the freshly-trained-to-kill.

"What's up, Meat?" he ribbed. "Good, Man, good- how's it going? You look totally ripped! How are they treating you?" "Three squares and all the rounds you can squeeze off! It's not so bad, once you settle in. But still, I can't wait to get to theater and start mowing." "Um, yeah. Cool. You're done in two weeks, huh? Then what?" "A cycle of combat jump school, four weeks of improv explosives training, and then I'm off to start making orphans." "Um, yeah. Cool, cool. You staying safe?" "Hell no- I'm staying dangerous!" And so it went. We spoke a bit more, trying on topics of home, but that world was too far away from him now; things like friends and girls were but waning memories and dangerous distraction to a mind needing its full force of focus for what was ahead. Our call ended abruptly, he being lured away by buddies on their way to town, presumably to test drive their new swagger on the lords and ladies of Killville. It was a disorienting call and there was obvious space between us- compounded by his newfound militancy. I didn't fault him for the distance or for his zeal. Something told me it was the safer way, the only way for him to get himself where he needed to be, so he could go do what he was about to do. But still, it was weird.

I don't know why, but it gave me a start to learn that my brother was everything I'd always known, but had never seen him to be. 'Track Your Hero' transmissions from the fighting zone told the story of a lion among men; an angel of death who prowled the front lines, stacking bodies and combat medals as so much cordwood. His killcam videos went viral, and quickly became the stuff of legend amongst battlefield soldiers and basement gamers, alike. Both parties were known to borrow his primal, "Gore and Glory!" battle scream anytime hope was fading and pluck was paramount.

His first combat scratch came in the form of having his arm blown off by a cluster round while taking a village in Sonora. The live-stream showed him leading a charge into a quagmire of smoke, rubble, and gristle. The explosion clouded the screen in a dusty pink mist that, once settled, revealed my brother writhing and screaming- one sleeve too many- before medics could drag him out and whisk him off to the nearest battlefield Refiguration Outpost. 200 hours later, he was back in the fight, the recipient of a new battle prosthesis and nearly three pounds of quantum-generated neo-tissue.

I didn't even know about the next injury until I saw him in person- home for R&R between his first and second tours. Six weeks prior, a fission grenade had relieved him of his left eye and most of that chiseled jaw: nothing that couldn't be replaced and upgraded by military largesse. Takes some getting used to, but once you have it down, the telescoping and night vision modes of the MOD3 Occu-Lens make you want to dig out your other eye and replace it, too. Or so I was told.

It was during this four week respite between deployments that I realized my brother had been killed in action, replaced with a lab-built and war-formed avatar. Combat-hardened muscles apart, he was physically about the same- it's a golden age of reconstructive technology. The change was manifest in his manner, and- if you happened to catch him unguarded- in the hollow look of his merely human eye.

He spent most of his time during those four weeks by himself: sleeping to mid-afternoon, walking long roads, eating little, drinking much. Never having had a nose for alcohol before, he'd picked up the scent since, and could now put down jugs of just about anything that burned without so much as a stumble or slur.

I ached to talk to him about something that mattered. To hear him, to be there for him- to connect, if even in the smallest way, like old times. I took his isolation and brooding for regret, for painful memory of the wreckage he'd been forced to create, but I was wrong. He wasn't brooding over the regret of war, he was hungering to return to it.

It was about a week before he shipped back to "the Zone" when he came by my room one morning and plunked down on the bed. We hadn't spent the weeks prior reveling in happy memory or running around town getting into hijinks together, like I'd daydreamed we would.

Our exchanges had been clipped and superficial, maybe intentionally so, neither of us knowing quite how to handle this new world view he'd been squeezed into. So his raw candor in this moment, apropos of nothing, caught me off guard: "It's strange being home, where everything is safe and easy. There's good food, soft beds, everyone is happy to see you. I should want to be here more than I do, but all I can think about is getting back to my buddies, back to the fight." "I don't want you to go back. I don't want you to get hurt anymore." "You know, it's funny- you get hurt once and you're scared to get hurt again. You don't want to go through it twice. But after you've been hurt twice, you stop being afraid of it. You develop a kind of shield from the fear. Killing is the same way- it gets easier the more you do it." Then without another word, he rose with his thoughts and left me to mine.

With a strained smile and feigned enthusiasm, I wished him well- off to his second round of war- a few days later. This was a much quicker tour. He wasn't three weeks in theater before his platoon wandered into an ambush and he took a hellacious hit that made a smear of him from the waist down. Even the pre-battle coagulating agent that all soldiers are pumped full of barely kept him alive before he could get to Refig. This time he got a full bionic mobility rig, along with a new set of lower body plumbing. Better than new and fully upgraded with all the best technology available- compliments of the geniuses that apply their prodigious intellects to the creation of such things.

Three hundred hours post-refig, as he's finishing accelerated restoration, my brother received the devastating news that he would not be returning to the fight. Though arguably the most battle-ready kill machine he'd ever been, given the extent of his aggregate injuries and subsequent reconstruction, he was now 73% neo-mass. This made him an incarnate violation of the Biomech Prohibition Clause of the Tehran Accords, stating no warfighter could be comprised of greater than 70% non-native components, lest they be considered Sentient Weaponry: "S-Dub" in war lawyer vernacular. So with little fanfare beyond the pinning-on of his third battlefield award for injury, and a "thanks for playing," my brother was unceremoniously discharged and mailed home: a military-grade weapon, deemed too dangerous for war.

I wish this was where the twist of the story came in. The part where after a few months of chopping wood in the mountains, my shirtless and bearded brother looks up to see intelligence officers hover-sledding into the meadow where he's working to recruit him for important, top secret work. The kind of work suited only to a combat veteran with a MOD3 Occu-Lens and bionic legs. Super action hero stuff.

Movie star excitement aside, I'd gladly settle for this part of the story being about my brother's uneventful return to peaceful quietude. The part where he learns to meditate, grows his hair long, gets a dog, comes to love woodworking: the embrace of a boring and beautiful life.

But instead, this is the part of the story where my brother returns home and bumbles aimlessly for months, scrounging just enough focus to increase his drinking tolerance and run off his girlfriend. It's the part of the story where his only outings are to the local war vet watering hole and his wage slave job as a part time night watchman at the edge-of-town scrap yard. In other words, this is the part of the story where I chronicle his sensationless decline.

The last conversation we had occurred the night before he wandered to the rail station, hopped a mag-train, and slid off over the horizon; accompanied only by his few possessions, which were stuffed into his battered War Force-issued rucksack. We met awkwardly in our parents' hallway, where I was on my way out to meet friends and he was on his way back from drinking, heading down to the basement for a bad night's sleep on the pullout sofa.

"Oh, hey!" I said- trying to sound enthused, but only coming across as startled. "Hey," his dead reply. He was clearly drunk- fabulously so- and had to lean against the wall to stay upright. "How's it going, Man? You in for the night?" I asked. "You know," he said, ignoring my small talk, "...it's damned lousy to be good at the thing you can't do. I'm a damned [burp] killing machine... who's gonna steal scrap [burp] metal?" "You ok?" I asked nervously. (he couldn't hear me) "There was a family in Hermosillo..." his gaze was over my shoulder, "...they were hiding in the back of a blown out restaurant..." (I didn't want to hear this) "...parents, three kids, abuela, a dog..." (he wasn't talking to me) "Let me take you downstairs, Man. Please." (I wasn't even there now, he wasn't either) "...the dog had to go- it was making too much noise..." (please stop) "the dad just kept saying, 'Tranquilo, por favor, tranquilo,' he was shielding everyone behind him..." (no) "...he was making too much noise, too..." (God, stop him) "... then they were all making too much noise." His dry and bloodshot eye never made contact. I was crying, trying to figure out what to say, how to respond to the greatest horror I'd ever heard. But he was already gone, stumble-falling down the stairs to the darkened basement below. Our final exchange.

I do my best thinking in the morning. I sit on the porch with my breakfast, wax poetic to myself, and sort through my stuff. With a little bit of quiet, seems there's very little I can't figure out in the light of the infant day. As I think now on my brother, I'm even able to marshal him into a loose index: the man he was, the things he took to war, the things war took from him, the misfortuned shell remaining.

Admittedly, I do sometimes hit a wall that can't be gone around- only over, or through. Like the one in front of me now: my own draft notice- the Order to Arms I received last night by digital courier. I can make no sense of the wave hitting me: punks, kiosks, neo-flesh, dogs, battle cries, Killville, girlfriends, basements, trains- all of it swarmed in a screaming cloud of pink mist.

The noise and chaos of it unstables me, and I beg counsel of the universe- how to summon the strength to answer this call without bursting into a thousand shards? A lonesome and sore-hearted voice echoes back: no one wins a fight.

****

Darcy Bayer

He loves games, my dad; always has. Sports games, word games, parlor games- he loves them all; is good at them, too. It took me to 12 to finally beat him at tetherball. I didn't best him at trivia until I was 23. I have yet to beat him at chess... There I go again. This is going to take some getting used to.

My dad has been dead for about six weeks now. I haven't quite yet adopted the past tense when thinking about him. Or talking about him. I know how this goes, though, so I'm sure it will work itself out. I got to practice on my mom. She died 10 years ago. I talked about her in the present for a long time, too. The grief-numbing disorientation eventually wears off, as all things do, with time.

Like I was saying, my dad loved games of all variety: sports games, word games, parlor games. His favorites were mind games. I don't mean that in the pejorative. I just mean he had fun with the tease. Riddles, pranks, and gags were his forte. For example, I was never *given* a present, I only ever found presents- usually with clues attending, but not always. Sometimes they'd be in the freezer, or on top of the roof, or strapped to the dog. You think I'm kidding. It took me a week to find my Christmas Wetty Betty doll when I was eight. It was in the basement in a box marked, 'Grandpa's ashes.' Dad had a dash of gallows humor in him- it added to the fun.

What really made Dad an elite prankster was his willingness to wait. He had the patience of a sniper. He'd put a prank in place and just let it sit, gestating, until it was all but forgotten. And then...gotcha! I remember after one summer when I was heading back to college, unbeknownst to me, Dad had sewn little tags into all of my underwear that read, 'Daddy's Big Girl.' Twisted, I know, but when eventually discovered-

and not by me, I might add- they achieved the intended effect. He was one of a kind. I really miss him.

Given Dad's penchant for tomfoolery, I should have been less surprised than I was when, 48 hours after his death, I received an unmarked envelope by courier containing three items: a sticky note with a phone number I didn't recognize, a small brass key hung from a silver chain and engraved with 'A-682,' and an old photograph of Mom, Dad, and me at the beach. The photo I did recognize. It was taken on a trip the three of us made to California when I was in high school. Mom and Dad have their arms around each other and I'm wedged between them. We're all smiling big. On the back of the photo- in Mom's hand- was written, 'Coronado Love- 2008.'

The number, it turns out, rang to the direct line of one Jennie Krause, Junior Vice President at Integrity First Bank & Trust. Among her myriad responsibilities, Ms. Krause oversaw apportionment of safe deposit boxes at this venerable house of lending. Ms. Krause, per Dad's antecedent provision, had been expecting my call, and assured me that safe deposit box A-682 was one under her purview. Inconveniently, as explained by Ms. Krause, safe deposit box A-682 could only be opened in person, and then only by the keyholder. Also inconvenient, as further explained by Ms. Krause, safe deposit box A-682 and the bank enclosing it were in Albuquerque, New Mexico. I live in Pittsburgh.

Dad's antics almost always involved some level of logistical complexity with little to no explanation, so this was not unfamiliar territory to me. Of course before I could tromp off to New Mexico and put a face to Ms. Krause's name, I had to first get through the loathsome task of shoveling the paperwork of the recently departed. I also had to bury Dad. As the only surviving member of our family triumvirate, these unenviable responsibilities fell to me. Thankfully, I had dreams of Albuquerque and Dad's last reveal to keep me inspirited through it all. I have little doubt the distraction was intentional, and meant to serve as an analgesic for the freshly-minted and reeling orphan I now was. Thanks, Dad.

Once the send-off was complete, the casserole dishes washed and returned, and the suspended silt of stirred grief had begun to float downward and settle, my mind cleared enough so that I could focus its energy on the divertissement of one last treasure hunt with Dad. Following a series of trains, planes, and hired cars, I arrived at the workroom of Ms. Krause: a tawdry, glassed-in cubicle that looked across the sparse vestibule and toward the hasteless teller windows of Integrity First of Albuquerque. Ms. Krause was mercifully taciturn and showed me to safe deposit box A-682 with friendly, but unceremonious efficiency. Her duties complete, with a smile and a nod Ms. Krause left me to my devices: the key around my neck, and the secret it was now to reveal.

With breath bated and hands shaking, I tilted the box up and toward me to see what my dad's farewell crack would be. I could almost hear his voice in my ear, "not so fast, Darce," as what slid out gave me a brief start, and then a knowing chuckle. Of course it wasn't going to be so simple as to receive a mysterious package, fly cross-country on faith and whim, drive to a random high desert bank, and collect your reward. Dad was a pro, and this was his final dance. What slid out was a single business card that read: 'UR Stuff Storage, 6839 E. Hummingbird Way, Scottsdale, Arizona. 24/365 access. Air-conditioned.' On the back of the card, Dad had written: '32-17-14, Unit 0211 No life without adventure. Almost there! XOXO Dad.'

I'll spare you the interlude between Albuquerque and Scottsdale. Suffice it to say it took a few more planes, trains, and hired cars to get me to Arizona, and more specifically, to the tiny manager's office of UR Stuff Storage, where Bart- the manager on duty- plied me with a complimentary bottle of water and a butterscotch from the communal dish, then directions to the elevator, the basement below, and storage unit 0211 within. Next, with a wave and a 'fare-thee-well,' Bart buzzed me through the security door, and into UR Stuff's steel-girded catacombs.

Judging by the nearly empty parking lot on my way in, there weren't many of us wandering these sterile, unpeopled halls, and sure enough, I didn't see anyone on my way down to Unit 0211, which I stood before- immobilized with nervous anticipation- for a solid 5 minutes prior to punching the combo, throwing wide the door, and entering upon Dad's Last Laugh.

It took a pause to understand what I was seeing.

Light from the hallway's fluorescent banks reflected into the metal cube- which measured 10 feet by 10 feet square- and illuminated the unit's lonesome dweller: a tumbled old stool- three-legged, wooden, and wholly nondescript. Atop the stool sat two envelopes: one, a large manila number typed "first" across it; the second, plain white and letter-sized, with "last" typed on its front. A closer view revealed the stool sat squarely over a large 'X' of blue painter's tape on the unit's concrete floor. X marks the spot: nice touch, Dad.

To say I had no idea what these envelopes contained is an understatement. To say I was nervous to find out, a grosser understatement still. But it seemed a shame to spend all that money on plane tickets and not find out, so with a steeling breath, I reached first for the manila envelope, undid its clasp, reached inside, and slid out that which was within.

As a kid, I always harbored a nagging suspicion that the King's men and their mounts hadn't tried quite hard enough before throwing in the towel on their efforts to refashion poor Mr. Dumpty. I get that fragile things fallen from a height make a pretty mess, but it seemed to me that when all the resources of a kingdom are brought to bear on a task- particularly one involving life and death- the outcome should produce better results than a collective throwing up of hands and hooves. These childhood suspicions were now confirmed by the tortured page that slid gingerly from the first envelope.

It was a typed letter on a single sheet of plain white paper. At some point, it had been torn to pieces. At some following point- long ago, judging by the brittle and yellowed tape that backed it- the letter had been painstakingly repieced into a Frankenstein version of its former- and miraculously still legible- self. Clearly a more patient effort than the one received by that ill-fated egg of yore. The letter read:

December 17, 2018

Charles Bayer
SVP, Operations
Eastern Associates, Ltd.
25065 N. Industrial Way
Pittsburgh, PA 15201

Mr. Bayer:

I'll forgo pleasantries. This letter serves to inform you of two things: first, of the death, by her own hand, of your former mistress- my mother- Margaret Bowen; and second, of the unpleasant truth that I am your biological son- sired by sin, then unwittingly raised as his own by a man of much greater character than yourself: my father.

I contact you now with no pleasure and no motivation, save one: it serves my mother's dying wish that you should know of my existence. Like you, I was enlightened of our connection only at the time of her passing. Do not regard this letter as any entreatment for further contact between us. I expect never to hear from you, nor should you expect ever again to hear from me. Your very existence is a stain I will work the rest of my life to scrub from my mind.

I have no doubt you are the halter that led my mother to her lonely and tortured end. As such, I will leave you with this earnest invocation to the powers that grant them: may life bestow on you everything you deserve, you son of a bitch.

The letter was unsigned.

Here was revealed Dad's prescience, as I surely would have collapsed onto the floor at this news, had there not been a stool for me to repair to. I sat numbly in that steel box, immersed in the white noise of shock for I don't know how long. I was outside of time. There was nothing to rouse me from my vacant reverie in that empty place- no noise of others, no hum of things, just a lonely girl far from home- a stranger in a strange land- sitting in silence amongst the shards of her shattered truth.

It was unrealistic to think that the good people at UR Stuff Storage would house me indefinitely though, so I eventually unblanked myself and turned my attention to that which in all the world terrified me most: the last envelope.

I opened it slowly, with unnecessary precision, trying comically to stall the unstallable. With sweat and tremble I drew out from the envelope the handwritten pages, as like a weapon from its sheath, and read:

My Darling Darcy,

First things first. I'm sorry for your loss. I'm sorry for how alone you feel right now. May it give you some small solace to know that we are never as alone as we feel. The world is rich with others, most of them strangers, but many of them friends. My dearest wish is that in this time of troubled waters, your ship may steer that safest harbor where love and loved ones await. May God bless your precious heart and your kind and gentle soul. I love you.

But maybe there's something else on your mind. Just maybe you are distracted by fresh revelation that things are not as you thought they were. For this I am sorry, too. Let me help make some sense of what you have just learned.

I'll say little of the affair, but that it happened- and ended- long, long ago. If you want details, they're easy to come by. Every song and story of love's pleasure and pain sings my soul. Nothing is more common to our condition on this earth, than the unknowable and untameable will of the human heart. I say this without any claim to innocence, only fallibility. These truths contain my greatest bewilderments, my greatest moments, my greatest shame.

When I received that letter many years ago, I read it in horror and destroyed it; then- like its author- I set myself to the task of forgetting. And I did. I immersed myself in everything that would help me unremember the misery and exultation of my ignominy. Time- that merciful salve- abetted. Your mother never knew of my betrayal. Or so I thought.

It's been my experience in this beautiful life that every heart harbors a darkest secret. If you don't have one yet, you may borrow this one until you find a suitable trade. I always thought the letter and the secret within was my darkest to keep, but I was mistaken. I found the letter amongst your mom's private things when she died, at the bottom of a box; buried beneath all the other relics. Turns out, this secret belonged to her.

I have no idea how she found the shreds of my lie, reconnected their pieces, and conjured the strength to never say a word. Or how she gifted me the silent grace to be flawed, to be flung against the rocks, then returned home- bruised and scarred- without so much as a query. Returned home into open and forgiving arms. Returned home to love, unconditional.

I tell you all of this not as some self-soothing deathbed confession, but with the hope that you might live in greater truth: we are all possessed of weakness, and of great strength, and of the need- most fundamental- for grace and love. It's a cruel irony that I must drag you through the pain of knowledge in order to deliver you to the doorstep of this wisdom. I hope the gift is worth the cost.

I love you, Darcy, my precious girl. Live a bold life. Be kind. Forgive. Love fearlessly. Your mom and I will see you soon, in Elysian fields- where we wait.

Love always,
Dad

No seat could steady me now, as the letter fell absently from my hand and beat me- but just- to the floor of this cruel cell, where I crashed, curled, and wept. Yes, the dike now broke- its flood released- and I wept. I wept for my dad's fragility, for his lover's pain, for her son's anger, and his father's strength. I wept for my suffered mother and the silent secrets she carried to her grave. I wept for the weakness, the passions, the cruelties, the losses, the rewards, the lies, the truths, and the love of all Mankind.

And then I wept for myself. For my loss, my loneliness, my innocence past. I wept and wept- racking, shoulder-wrenching sobs- until my eyes swelled shut and my cheeks soaked wet. I wept until the weeping was done. And then I stopped.

As I lay there on the cold floor- my breath settling, my wits returning- a calm visited me, and a small voice spoke- so still that had I not been in that silent and solitary place, I would have missed it: You're ok, Darcy. It will all be ok.

Somewise, these simple words of truth restored me. Wiping my eyes, I rose and left my cage, grabbing Dad's letters on the way. Up the elevator and out the door, I stepped from the building and into the desert sun's light- white and piercing- as so much blinding knowledge. Then I tossed the manila envelope and its re-torn contents into a bin, called for a car, and hopped a plane to Pittsburgh.

****

campfire tale

Far back ten hundred years ago- before the yoke of steel, when crop and tide marked time, and tribes humbled knowledge to wisdom- a trail was marked through these parts by the ancient courageous. Tooled only with sinew, stick, and stone, for five generations the mountain clan hewed and hacked a path- two horses wide- through the thin-aired pass of primeval wood and gibber plain that fortressed one side of the range from its other. Years stretched to decades as the path footslogged its way up, through, and over the impenetrable parts; the best of each brood being sent to serve the trail that their toil untwined. It was risk-ridden work consigned only to the most honorable braves, as fewer ever returned than went, and those that made it back came always with tales to tell.

There are many ways to die on the path: falling stones, falling men, and hungry beasts claim their share, but nothing instills terror in intrepid hearts as does the wood demon. A soul-seeking spirit that was vexed awake by bygone men with hammer and ax, it prowls the high pass and lies in wait for the unwitting. To walk this road is to cross its lair, and here is where you find it: as the trail makes its highest point, from the trees the path emerges into a stone-strewn and too-silent glade where an alpine stream beckons the weary to repose. But linger not long- so tell the braves- for here the devil preys. And should you meet it, be warned: it takes no steady shape, but changes as it will to the form that serves best its cravings. So hold your breath, if pass you must, for if you're seen, you'll never be found...

****

As any worthy raconteur will attest, the campfire glow lends an illusion of boundary to those within its orange dome from the deathblack darkness of the wilderness without. In steady hands, this semblance of safety can give listeners a friendly spook without plunging them into the terror of their truth: total and defenseless isolation. Dr. Winston understood this well and used it to his good advantage as he regaled round the flickering flame his three traveling companions with the legend of the trail they had these five days trod, the forest they would tonight sleep within, and the high saddle glade they would tomorrow traverse.

But this was not a company quick to scare. Seasoned trailhands all, the four friends and their horses had set out a week past from the lonesome cowboy outpost of Goodbye Gulch in search of deep wilderness, and- if fortune favored- maybe an elk or ram. They were armed and provisioned, well-prepared for the expedition, and experienced enough to handle a contingency or two.

Horses bedded, chow ate, bottle passed, and stories told, it was time to bunk down and rest to dawn. So beneath the quilt of a billion stars, they slept and dreamt the sleep and dreams of the fatigued and much-contented.

Jackson Rue rose in silence with the dull glow of predawn to set the fire, fry the rashers, and boil the grounds. He was a wizard with a hot camp pan, and nearly as good on the jaw harp. Cap Allen woke next to feed and water the mounts. He could hit a bird's eye at a thousand yards- a trick he picked up sniping unlucky foes during the war. Henry George and Dr. Winston roused last. Doc wandered off to make water, while Hank hobbled over to Jackson to welcome him to the day and have a cup. His limp the result of an ill-placed blade through the foot during a drunken game of mumbly peg on another ride with the boys years back. After vittles they broke camp, saddled up, and sifted onto the trail in loose formation: Doc riding point, Cap next, then Hank and Rue.

Talk comes slow on a long ride and a man finds himself on the trail with lots of time to think. Ideas amble in and out as you acquire a sort of meditative state, and settle into the rhythm of your surroundings. The clop of hooves, the squeak of saddle leather, the soft mumblings of a man deep in thought billow and swirl amid the shrieks of high-up hawks, and wind through trees; all arrange to different sections of the same symphony. It's a pleasant place to pass the time, an easy place for the mind to wander.

And so it happened as the horsemen rode on- sloping uptrail like as on a languid swell, each encased in his own reverie- that they were ungently knocked from their engrossments when they rounded a bend and uponed to a misplaced scene.

It seemed at first some wrong-colored stone had rolled onto the trail, the red and black not nature made. As the foursome approached, a closer view revealed not a stone, but rather a heaped up form garbed in denim and buffalo plaid, acting the way a dead man might, which is to say- a moveless lump of lifeless meat. Its hatless head was covered in a tangled mess of straw blond hair. The face was not revealed.

Hopping nimbly from his mount, Doc was first to approach and there to find a slack and stock-still child. His breath came small and rasping, but come it did, though this is where the good news ended and hope gave way to horror. Trussed tightly- round throat to boot- the boy was mummy-wrapped in rusty barbed wire- it burrowed through his clothes and sank into the flesh below. He was slick with blood and had been dumped without ceremony where he lay. Best guess put him around eleven or twelve years aged.

Moving with grim efficiency as like the seasoned surgeon he was, Doc turned the boy to his back, grabbed the lineman's pliers from his saddlebag, and began to cut and dislodge strands of corroded metal from the near-dead child. The other men dismounting next, took Doc's cue, grabbed their tools and began cutting, too. The boy's eyes looked up into his skull and showed only white. Foam bubbled pink at the corner of his mouth.

As the stiffless sufferer was slowly unfettered and his bonds unbound, blood flowed the greater, but his breath improved. Doc implored a quick encampment so their patient could be made stable and put to more thorough ministration. Fortune shone down, as Cap rode ahead then back, reporting a nearby clearing with a soft creek flowing through. The riders made haste, their patient in tow.

It was a sleepless night as Doc directed the men around the fire to various tasks in service to their slow-stabilizing victim. Water was fetched and boiled, bandages wrapped, changed, then re-wrapped, and a vigilant watch kept over breath and bleeding. When finally dawn crept in, the worst was through and survival now a cautious expectation. Rue's coffee never tasted so good.

It was late into the next day when the boy began to stir from his restless sleep. His eyes fluttered briefly then flashed open in panic, the wide-eyed terror reminiscent of a bog-trapped foal. He struggled to rise, but the riders held him down- a surprisingly difficult task; the boy was strong with fear.

"Where am I? Who are you? I gotta get off this mountain! Lemme go!" The boy was panicked, nearing hysterics, thrashing against the arms that held him. "There's a devil roams here! A soul taker! I'm the last of us! Blest heaven and tarnation, we gotta go! Lemme go!" More thrashing. "Easy, Son, easy," Doc soothed as he tried to calm his discomposed patient. "You're safe, you're ok now. Here, have a drink," Doc motioned to Hank for a canteen. The boy took the water absentmindedly, sipped small, then- seeming to regain some wit- met eyes with his benefactors, who were circled tightly around him.

"This wood is spoilt, evil like. We gotta go." With greater control, but still terror-stricken, the boy spoke more slowly, on a knife's edge of frenzy. Rue asked gently, "Who did this to you? Where are they now?" "Ma and Pa got took... Baby too. Why did it took the baby?" His moment of lucidity gone, the boy began to slide back to his dark hysteria.

Having seen war, Doc and Cap knew well the look of unbridled panic a man's eyes can take when losing his grip on what's real. Rue knew that face as the one his father flashed him before the Tulsa roughs slid a loop over his head and lifted him by his neck up a tree, some thirty years back. Hank was a man of the range and- by appointment- only too familiar with the varied decorations of primal fear. None of the men, however, had ever stood in the presence of such gross insanity, as like that to which they now bore witness.

Water didn't calm him, so they moved to whiskey, and after a wee dram the boy's story began to trickle, then flow:

"We was three of us riding westbound by horse-drove wagon outta Mizzoura- Independence town- heading to Eureka Valley in San Fran-fer to 'stablish Pa's mercantile. There was Pa, me, 'an Ma. Ma was 'spectant with a little 'un so we was rushin' to git round the range 'fore first snow hit. Bad fer us tho', the wagon wer too heavy 'an we sunk 'er in soft sand, west 'a Kamas. Pa got real nervous, cuz he didn't wanna have no baby in tha mountain winter, so we cut the Conestoga loose an' tried to make fast on horseback straight o'er the pass 'fore real cold hit.

"We was bout five days up mountain- things going good- when we met a hitch. Coming round a blind turn, we troubled a sow griz with a couple a cubs. She didn't like it none and made to charge, but then veered off into the woods with her little ones at the last chance. We was scared good, but none chewed up, thanks to Heaven. One of our horses spooked though- got hisself twisted up and busted a leg. We knowed we had to put 'im down, though Pa had that mama griz on his mind. By the time we gits ourselves resi-tiated it was getting on to late day and we didn't have much trail light left. Not wanting to bring round another meeting on account a the blood smell, and specially not at dark, Pa decided we'd make camp and set up a big fire and a perimeter, then get on early next morning and leave the carcass behind.

"So we moves a little uptrail, away from the remains, til we find a campable clearing- bit rocky, but had a waterin' crick- and we lodge down for the night. Made us a big fire, passed round some hardtack for supper, then put our backs to the flame and Pa an' me kept a two man rifle watch while Ma got some rest. 'Ventually, all goes to calm, no bear in sight- and Pa and me each settled in with hisself.

"Must have been 'bout halfway to sun up when everything goes real quiet. Too quiet fer forest. Even the crick seemed to stop bubbling. It was real dark, too, on account a there being no moon that night an plenty a clouds. There weren't no treeline to our eyes neither, just one big sheet a black outside the fire's glow. Felt like what deaf and blind must feel like, I 'magined to misself. Both of us was a little tight, thinking that mama sow must be nosing near about. Then the noise starts up, real quiet like.

"Twas a moanin' sorta sound- but part growl, too. Ain't neither of us could tell where the sound was coming from, seemed to be surrounding us from the whole wood at once- everywhere and nowhere. Sound starts gittin' louder and we can tell it ain't no bear, but somethin' else- not quite man, an' not quite natural. Sorta lonely and threatenin'. Ma's up by now too, gittin' real nervy, and hollers who's there, and Pa tells her to hush up. It don't stop the sound, though, fact it starts gittin' louder.

"We's all gittin' pretty twitchy by this time, sitting in dark black as sleep, and hearing whatever we's hearing surrounding us, when from what musta been the wood's edge, a small glow starts up and we source the sound to it. Weren't much shine to start with, but after a bit we can tell it's two blue lights- bright an small, close together an comin' toward us slow.

"The blue lights is moving closer an closer, that moaning sound all the while accompanin', then as it's all gittin' close to the edge of the campfire rim, of a sudden the lights go out and the sound goes off. Everything is back to quiet and dark."

As if by way of demonstration, the boy at this went death silent and stone still. He sat for a moment, deep in muted thought, seeming by appearance to be gathering the resolve to continue his account. His strength regained, with a fortifying breath, the boy resumed:

"Can't right say what happened next- all fell to chaos. What I seen is a devilbeast step from tha dark an' into tha' light, its eyes bluer 'n blazin' blue. Like sapphires on fire. Didn't right knowed what I was lookin' at. Ma starts a screamin' but gets cut off short on account a' havin' tha baby tore out her belly by that monster, who moves faster 'n anything I ever seen. Pa fires off a shot, tho' ain't nothin' to hit but air. Then somethin' from the edge of the firelight grabs him from behind an' yanks 'im away, screaming into the darkness. In no seconds time, I'm there by misself- Ma an Baby is on the ground- bled out limp, and Pa is flat disappeared 'n not screaming no more. Then I hears that moanin' growl behind me, and all goes dark. That's last I remember, 'fore seeing y'all."

At this the boy laid back, exhausted by the labor of recount, and shut his eyes in rest.

Next to the campfire's low embers and dying flame the shaken riders left the child to sleep, moving into the stony glade, where small light from the moon's waning crescent played strange with shadow- the last of day having departed since the story's start. Their eyes spoke first, as they each asked the other with a brittle look, "What now?" Hank was first to break the silence, "We gotta take that boy and get outta here quick." Cap added what all were thinking but none were inclined to say, "...'fore it gets us, too."

As the four friends hunkered in the rocky soil scratching a plan of escape, a low and rising sound started up that froze the brave mens' blood. It was one part moan to two parts growl- forlorn and angry- and it seemed to enfold the meadow where they sat. The plan was quickly ditched, as all thoughts distilled to one: get out.

The riders rushed back to the campsite to grab the boy and escape. They found him, to their surprise, not lying in rest, but standing near the dying embers, shirtless and bloody bandaged- his tortured back faced to their return. The moaning growl had ceased.

"We gotta get gone, Son. Right now. Something's out there," Doc spoke with hurry. The boy seemed neither to hear, nor care. He stood immobile toward the fire, his savaged back still turned.

"I 'preciate y'all fixin' me up," he spoke to the men but into the dark. "Thought fer sure I was a goner. Gotta tell ya, I'm feelin' a right sight better." He was motionless, his front and hands hidden. "Glad to hear that, Son..." said Doc cautiously, "...though I think you'd be better-suited to take more rest. You aren't healed up enough to move about yet. That aside, we gotta go. Now."

"Wish I could..." said the boy, his back still turned, "...but 'fraid I gotta be headin' on- other travellers to meet, ya know. 'Fore I go, though, I reckon a proper introduction would be fittin'. Now I knows Doc, 'n Rue, n' Hank, n' Cap, but I don't reckon y'all knows me."

Uncertain silence sat over the fear-frozen men.

"There's some calls me, 'Old Nick' and others, 'Old Ned'. A few from way back even calls me, 'Mr. Black,' or, 'The Great Deceiver'. And I goes by a legion a other names, too. But what I'm most familiar by ain't my name, so much as my trade. And here it is..."

At this, the boy turned to face them as the very last of the embers died, and the four riders were pitched into unsighted darkness. First thing the men discerned was that the boy's hands- which he held palms-up and waist-high before him- were glowing blue. Each hand held a marble- shooter sized- that blazed like a flaming gem and cast a spectral glow in a small ring around him. His bare and bandaged chest had two black stripes running vertically down it. The men's eyes drew upward from the blue-glowing orbs, past the dark stripes, and up into the boy's shadowed face. They recoiled in icy terror. His eyes were dead black craters- raw empty holes- and it was quickly clear that the stripes were blood trails running down wet from the ragged sockets. Following the bloody tracks down the boy's slight frame, the men realized with horror that the blue orbs weren't marbles at all, but the boy's own eyes, blue as a glacier lake. They were alert and leering hungrily upon each of the riders in turn. The cowboys were terror-struck, as the devil with a hellborn shriek sprung upon them in a lightning strike of blinding blue...

And so as it had for a thousand years, the forest swallowed the screams of these poor, damned souls, who found too late that they had wandered into the wood demon's still and stony prowl. Once the blood curdles died and their echoes receded, then- as like a serpent just struck- the freshly hushed greenwood re-coiled itself to a loose repose, and the alpine glade of Devil's Pass returned to silence- sitting in wait for its next misfortuned passerby.

****

600 words

100
Sometimes I don't like to watch old footage of beautiful, talented folk because it reminds me that eventually, everyone's train stops rolling. Eventually, we're forced to recycle old memories, because we stop making new ones. But other times I draw inspiration from seeing replayed that moment of a life achieving its pinnacle. These souls call to me, saying, "See this thing I did? See this thing I made? You do it, too. But hurry- you'll be dead soon." And then I feel like a God blessed lion and jump back in, returning to work- erecting my own Monument to Was.

200
Larches lose their needles even when the other pine trees don't. What an apostate- that libertine larch. Imagine the courage it takes to stand in a vast forest of others like you, and be the only one willing to disrobe. Do you think they like it: standing there, bare branched to the snow, scoffing down the green and sharp leafed woods? What a fearless life, to live a larch. Such noble and reaching things- it makes one wonder: Do you think they think? Like, I wonder if they wonder what it's like to be us. They're probably above it all.

300
Don't be disturbed, but I can't deny the small part of me that wants to jump- right over the side, down the dam, and into the rocky tailwater below. It must be that gene I hear we all possess: the tiny self destruct button that lies within our breast, encased within a protective aegis of sensibility. Realistically, the chances of me popping over the rail and down are about 96% against; for all intents and purposes, a true impossibility. But yet, something prevents me from saying definitively that it won't happen. What an odd thing it is to need uncertainty.

400

There's a dead eyed look assumed by those who have resigned themselves to their fate. Like all their promise has faded, and any hope of adventure, gone. It shows up in so many ways: a milquetoast profession, a drug addict kid, a bleeding limping love affair- the list goes on. I saw it today in the eyes of a woman at the DMV. Her gaze screamed such apathy- she seeped ennui and loss- and I wondered if the genesis was perhaps something more foundational to her life than just the government wait. After surveying the line, I decided- probably not.

500

Lotsa people hear 'soulmate' and reckon the lovers must have it all smooth and cozy. I can tell you it ain't like that. Sure there's heaps a' happy- a luvin' spirit who knows you real good makes it that way. But this here's a battlefield- thar's demons' trouble and the Devil's mischief everywhere. It's real quick to get in crosswise, so you gotta keep a sharp look. That's where a soulmate earns its keep. Ain't so much in the clear skies, as it is in the trenches- under the falling hot metal- when you most need yer All Of It.

600

What a thing it must be- to see everything in black and white. Bit bland perhaps, but certainly not all bad. Maybe the lack of color imbues an appreciation for texture. How things *feel*, you know? By seeing less, you intuit more. And maybe one looks farther- down toward some away, long distant point- for lack of a distracting hue. I live my life in greens and blues. And sometimes shades of brown. It's a grand palette and one I wouldn't trade. Not even for the far seeing, laser precision of black and white. I'd miss the trees too much.

****

I sit in the lobby

I sit in the lobby of a once-opulent playground. I used to come here in the Before- lived right around the corner, in fact. I'd ride bikes over with my wife and kids. We'd spend weekend days lunching and swimming in the resort's massive network of interconnected pools: waterfalls, waterslides, grottoes, the whole shebang. Sometimes we'd get a room and stay overnight; in the parlance of the time, what was called a "staycation." Very clever, very indulgent. An alien concept in this, the new real: the After. The venue still stands, though the pools are long gone- commandeered by quarantine officials for use as mass graves during the Sickness. Defunct outcroppings of plaster-stone abut cement footprints- pool-shaped, like a detective's chalk outline- the only demarcations now of the swimming hole's former trace. I'm told the youngish anymore use the flat surfaces for springtime bonfires, but I take it at word. I know a few people under that concrete, and I'd glean no pleasure from walking atop it.

Nature has reclaimed the sprawling grounds. Some folks scrounge the now-wild footpaths and desiccated fairways in search of rabbits, lizards, snakes. Fresh meat is nice, but I limit my foraging to cans, vacuum packs, and jars; call me lazy. Plus, if- like me- you have a memory for what was here before, seeing what's here now only serves to stir up thoughts best left unstirred. I wander no further than the lobby these days.

In its glory, the lobby was two stories tall of sunlit crystal, cashmere, marble, music, fountains, flowers, and art. No price too high to deliver the experience of ultimate luxury. Richly polished woods, exotic weaves, fashions of the moment abounded, and everywhere rang the silent screams of understated affluence. North and south walls of floor-to-ceiling glass. The former facing crags of the desert mountain against which this place was built, the latter facing out and down to the pools, the golf course beyond, and the shimmering city oasis yet beyond. Dotted across the foyer's vast carpeted landscape was a panoply of deep sofas, chairs, and low slung tables, loosely hemmed into intimate clusters by verdant perimeters of potted palms and ferns: perfect for barely-seen-and-never-overheard tête-à-têtes. Offset in the southwest quadrant was the lobby's crown jewel: a circular bar, sunken three steps deep from the main floor, its surface of translucent stone underlit and ethereally aglow. Clear and amber potables of all variety here served, along with a list of gooey blender drinks long as your arm, all meant to set mind and tongue to buzz.

The lobby looks quite different now.

What's gone: but for the highest-hung, most of the art. Flammables- including every wood panel, sheet of paper, menu, magazine, napkin, pencil, side table, book, manual, curtain, carving, coffee cup, combustible objet d'art... you get it. Those springtime bonfires are hungry affairs. All lamps- table and floor; every drop of juice, booze, water, and beer. Cutlery. Glasses. Plates and platters. Electronics- televisions, phones, computers, cash registers, printers; the like.

What remains: the hotel's formerly-iconic-now-dust-drenched cut glass chandelier. Most sofas and chairs- though the illusion of viridescent intimacy has departed upon death by disregard of many a palm and fern. Only a smattering of unkillables persist- limp drooping in their chipped and paint-faded pots. Remnants from the wide meadow of once-rich carpet, now threadbare and intermittently moistened by spillage and neglect. This place is tired- true- but it's not yet gone to sleep.

A brief pause to laud Humanity.

One could hardly be blamed for thinking that given society's pre-Sickness fascination with eschatological chaos, when something "bad" did actually happen, we'd all lose our minds, and plunder and pillage our way to extinction. I gladly report, this did not happen. Yes, there was some initial panic; yes, a few windows were broken, a few stereos lifted; yes, the occasional maiden did meet with unpleasantness at the tine's tip of the occasional rapist; but did civilization collapse? No.

Did the cities burn? No. Did ruin reign? Emphatically, no. In truth, we all kept a pretty clear head. It helped that the Sickness raged like wildfire, killing quickly and cleanly, leaving in its wake a still functioning and largely automated world, capable of providing a but-only-lessened level of convenience to a now much smaller contingent: the Immune Remainder. We didn't run out of food, fuel, or water; we ran out of people. Back to the lobby...

I doubt I'll ever tire of seeing human resourcefulness in action. Indeed, that candle burns brightest in the deepest dark. To wit, as the Sickness petered and those of us left were reeling in the wake of what to do next with all this stuff, it occurred to seemingly everyone that the nicest of our new things ought to be repurposed to support the utilitarian needs of those rattling around in the After. Sensible sedans were swapped for sports cars, apartments for mansions, and staid coffee shops for opulent resort lobbies. Though none among us seem to have the energy or inclination to maintain the world's former grandeur, turns out many enjoy sitting in splendor amongst the gradually flaking gilt and the slow souring wine of the Coming-To-Pieces. I place myself firmly in that camp, as I lounge here now in my favored chair, with its favored vantage of a slow-moving assemblage ensconced in a space of decadent decline.

There are two sitting apart at the bar: one nosed in a book, the other gazing off with vacant stare holding a fork above a tin of half-eaten ravioli- some thought having seemingly stalled him mid-bite. Another in a corner plays checkers with herself. She thinks hard, makes a move, spins the board. Repeat. Resources are abundant in this age, and commerce is all but dead. Some play the game still, though; call it, "For Old Time's Sake." There are three at it over by the dry fountain, two in a bidding war for the third's something-or-other. Fistfuls of hundreds are animatedly waving about. The stakes are nothing. Across the room, against the wall in facing chairs over a table, two men are engaged in some seemingly friendly, but intense dialogue. There is a familiarity to their gestures suggesting old acquaintances in present reunion. My regard is aroused.

Why notable, you ask? It's rare in this place that life from the Before is remet with life in The After. Everyone here- and I mean Everyone- has lost their treasures. Whole networks wiped out: parents, spouses, children, siblings, friends, lovers, acquaintances, familiar strangers. Three of every thousand survived. And while over time, we- the Remainder- managed to recluster into loose bands, as our kind is wont to do, a certain amount of space is maintained. Yes, we like to be *around* one another, but no longer *together* with each other. The lingering memory of so many severed connections- so much love lost- keeps the wounds raw. On one view, the most acute casualty of the Sickness was not the lost lives of those departed, but the lost intimacy between those remaining.

I wonder on these two. What topic could elicit such intensity between them? Passions in this time are widely muted; there's been too much loss, the tanks are dry. The future is a topic too unprecedented to engender heated emotion, the present is too disorienting to abide meaningful study. That leaves only the minefield of the past: dangerous, but emotive. These men and their casual discou...

[glimpse-flash-behind sofa-where did]

****

"...stayed at home, armed and ready in May. I ventured a little in June, mostly for water. Thank God it didn't go to July, we were getting dry and thirsty," says the first man. "We were lucky in that," agrees the second man.

Surely in some dusty library on some dusty campus in some dusty college town there's a dogeared tome that explains the psychology that incites the Immune to share their personal exploits from the Eight Week Chaos: the early, first, and only mass panic during the Sickness. Maybe it's the low hanging fruit of shared experience- like veterans talking bootcamp- a never fail icebreaker. Maybe it's survivor's guilt and the need to explain to any captive audience that there was nothing to be done- it came on so fast. Maybe it's just good old fashioned catharsis; a story shared for the sake of the teller rather than the listener. Whatever human complexity undergirds the motivation, seems these days all conversations between any stranger-cum fellow well-met begins with the credential exchange of what you did during "The Eight."

"I thought we were well-prepared, but I didn't expect the ferocity," the second man speaks softly. "Mmm hmm," the first nods and grunts in understanding. "I was caught in public when it broke. Should have stayed in, of course, but I was so tired of the chatter by then. The hysteria seemed put on- I didn't trust the media; their 'end is near' rhetoric just wasn't playing for me. At least not that day." "Mmm hmm," the first encourages. "So I decided to pop out for one more round of supplies- always need water in the desert, right? I was walking into the grocery- almost to the door- when I see a lady walking out like casual. I wouldn't have even noticed her, but for the fact that she wasn't wearing her vent-gear. So she caught my eye. Then I noticed she had an ice pick sticking out of her throat, all the way to the hilt. Strangest of all, she was just walking along like everything was good. And then, as she passes me, she gives me a thumbs up. Can you imagine?" "Bizarre." "You have no idea. Then she walks for another 10 feet or so, and collapses. Face down onto the pavement- no hands out, nothing to break her fall, just- bam(!)- face first. Then nothing. I was in shock. Stood there trying to process- probably for just a second, but it felt like a day. As I'm standing there- too scared to touch her- the shots start and the whole store comes emptying out. I didn't know what was going on, but I knew it wasn't good. So I run like hell back to my car. I had a close spot- I was lucky. I jump in, and pull out fast. I turned the wheel too hard, though, and hit the guy next to me. I'm scraping down the side of this truck, people are running around everywhere now- yelling, crying, shooting- it was like a fuze that everyone was waiting on had just been lit. Straw that broke the camel's back, whatever. Things just exploded in a moment." "Mmm hmm." "So anyhow, I'm scraping down the side of this truck, pedal down just trying to get out of there, and I hit...something. Back right over it, front tires, too. [pause] And I just keep going, hit two or three more cars on the way out. I get out of the parking lot and blast towards home. The roads were already insane- people driving like maniacs, running lights, hitting each other. Our house was only a few blocks from the store, but I almost didn't get there. Someone tried to shoot out my tires at an intersection- got one of them. I was running on a rim by the time I got home, sparks flying everywhere." [long pause]

[Quietly, more exhale than spoken word] ("i didn't even look to see what i ran over- just kept going to get out of there, fast as i could. for a long time i told myself it was a dog. it wasn't a dog.")

****

I wonder on these two. What topic could elicit such intensity between them? Passions in this time are widely muted; there's been too much loss, the tanks are dry. The future is a topic too unprecedented to engender heated emotion, the present is too disorienting to abide meaningful study. That leaves only the minefield of the past: dangerous, but emotive. These men and their casual discou...

[glimpse-flash-behind sofa-where did]

Something in my periphery distracts. A too-small man drunkenly totters into the corner of a sofa, bumps against it, then stumbles behind it- just beyond my sight. That can't be right. Not that there aren't plenty of drunks around these days, but the proportions are off- the man is too small- the lack of logic affronts. I tear my attention away from the talking men, in search of the stumbling drunk. Ha! This is no drunk- it's a child, a toddler more specifically, of just-learning-to-walk age, bumping itself around the room. If a monkey on horseback came through the lobby right now, it would be only slightly less strange.

Far between are children in this time. Though many were immune, few survived. Without parents, family, or friends, the Dependent and Unattended were made quick work of by Death's blind and wide-swinging scythe. Tragic in the abstract, but in the trenches of the Sickness, unless it was your kid...meh. Like I said, the tanks ran dry.

What makes this kid doubly strange is the fact that given its age, it's clearly a child of the After. Of course we still have the technology to make babies- it's just that we largely don't. The flesh functions, but the heart and mind are barren. To quote a wiseman, "the thrill is gone." Also strange, a quick scan of the room suggests- beyond me- no one is taking any interest in this kid. By all appearances, it's stumbling and bumping around on its own.

There was a time when triggers were everywhere. A sound, a smell, an otherwise benign object- anything could trip the wire and set memory off in your face like a bomb. Nothing more dangerous than the implements of childhood: parks, toys, colors, small things- it took next to nothing to flip the switch. God help you if you saw a picture of a child, or worse yet- an actual child. Once ago, if this kid had wandered past me, I'd be wrapped around myself in a sobbing ball. But as I sit here now, seeing it teeter around- pacific and ill-protected, I feel... beige. What's worse I can't say: to be enwreathed by the catalysts of pain, or to numbly subsist in a twilight of indifference.

As it bangs and bumbles about, it occurs to me that this kid is the unwitting agent of wisdom, and an exemplar of a universal truth: if we don't look out for each other, we are all of us in existential peril. Used to be, together we formed interlocking webs, now we free float like electrons- gently orbiting and slightly repelling one another. How in this lonely new world do we generate enough energy to care and connect?

Someone must be looking for this kid. A more earnest attempt to locate its steward convinces me it's- impossibly- here by itself. Another peculiar effect of life in the After is that the extraordinary is now commonplace, and the impossible merely extraordinary. So while nature prohibits the absurdity of sow-less cubs, like the one right in front of me, I'm less bothered by this paradox than you might expect. But I am starting to feel a clinical curiosity creep in, if for no other reason than it lets me dodge a little boredom in the interest of seeing what happens next.

The kid is patient, if nothing else. It takes a few steps, falls down, gets up, a few more steps, bumps into something, falls down, gets up, immediately falls down again, gets up, et cetera. It's exhausting to watch, but impressive- the kid never loses its cool, just keeps falling and getting up- learning with each step and making slow but steady progress across the wide lobby floor.

A decision point: left toward the sunken bar, or right toward the open front entrance? Brief deliberation (what tyro logic commands that blank slate?) then, right. Wobble, wobble, wobble... almost to the door... wobble, wobble... at the door... wobble... out the door. Roll me in flour and call me a biscuit if that kid didn't just pop out of nowhere, wander the lobby, and walk right out the front door, without anyone so much as looking at it. God bless the After.

Hard-boiled cynic that I am, my inclination is to watch the kid go, reflect self-indulgently on the insanity of humankind, and go about my day. Curious and sentient ape that I am, another inclination is to follow it out and watch the show- maybe get the chance to be taught a lesson about danger at another's expense.

But what's this? There's a third inclination- fomented in some deep recess, some dark corner of a long-past, far-ago life: the urge to protect this child, to help him. These are strange thoughts, but what can I do- the human pull is there. Growing, in fact, gaining life as I give it attention. What might happen if rather than gawk or ignore, I engage? "No!" memory and pain scream back at me. "Remember what happened last time!" "Yes!" retorts some still, small voice. "Risk and seek your reward!" I'm immobilized by the debate. Every second I sit, the child wanders farther afield, toward who knows what lot.

Some outer-body urgency gives me my answer, enjoins me to stand, and commands me to follow, and save. So I do: up from my battered chair, across the soiled space, past the broken & motley set, and into the out-of-doors.

****

7

Throughout my formative years and into early adulthood, the sum total of what I knew of my paternal grandfather, The Right Reverend Chip Thwayt, condensed to 3 tidy bites. 1st, he was a theologian of global renown and a bishop most-esteemed, of the High Temple Mythos. 2nd, his suicide- that occurred 4 years before my birth- was shrouded in suspicion and at the time lay thick with ecclesiastic intrigue; understandable circumstances considering how the pronounced 'self-inflicted' gunshot wound that killed him exited through his chest. And 3rd, Brother Chip- as he was widely known- could write in perfect cursive with either hand- a talent he would gleefully demonstrate anytime for anyone who asked.

Now while this isn't much information to build any kind of meaningful image of a grandparent off of, I did my best, and spent many years and untold hours speculating on the details of this colorful man's life. Having few actual facts to work with allowed me the creative latitude to design his avatar to my will. I imagined him to be a person of idiom and charm. People (in my mind) were drawn to his unabashed humor and seldom-unsunny demeanor; drawn like fish to an angler's torch. He was magnanimous and kind; he was stentorian and droll. He was (in my mind) a great conversationalist. I thought of all the things we would have talked about together and all the things he would have taught me, had we had the chance. We were real pals. In my mind.

I recently came into another shot of information on the man, which helped me to distill some spirit of fact from the mash of fiction. It was 2 days past my 34th birthday when I had the pleasure of visiting with my beloved Great-grandaunt Trudy, Brother Chip's only sibling, whom I had met for a belated birthday lunch of enchiladas and iced tea at Don Jose's- our favorite cantina and meeting place.

Aunt Trudy had always been reticent to discuss Chip, a fact I attributed to the never-healed wounds of her brother's provocative passing, and it was a topic that I had long ago learned to avoid. So it was some kind of surprise to me when, after having ordered our lunch, she slid an age-beaten shoebox across the table and bid me open it. Inside sat a perfectly round piece of polished obsidian- golf ball sized, mirror-finished, and blackest black. Next to the glass stone was an audio chip and player labeled: *Sermon of 7 (delivered 01/25/26, Bozeman diocese).* I was befuddled by the box and its contents, and my expression must have shown it.

"Happy Birthday," Trudy said to me smilingly. "Uh, thanks," I replied uncertainly, "what is it?" "Just some old stuff of your grandpa's that I had hanging about. I thought you might find it interesting," she replied. I looked at her expectantly, hoping she would expound. "The rock is your grandpa's seer stone. The magic died with him, of course, but I thought it might make you an interesting paperweight. The recording is an old homily," she continued, "remnants from his days in Montana." "Cool- thank you!" I said, and meant it. "Give it a listen and see what you think. If nothing else, at least you'll get a taste of Chip in his element," she added with a tone of finality, then steered our conversation to a different course.

Later that night, after kicking off my boots, then packing and lighting my pipe, I pulled the audio player out of the shoebox and hit 'play' on the chip, palming the stone and mindlessly running my thumb across its flawless surface as I listened. An unfamiliar voice spoke. It was buttery and baritone; presumably my Grandpa Brother Chip:

"May the goddesses and gods of Mythos steer our minds and lead our hearts as we meditate on their divine teachings. In the name of the Great Temple we pray, so let it be." Then the man's words were met with a resounding, "Let It Be!" from the congregation, and I could hear on the recording the clump and shuffle of the worshipers as they dropped onto their pews en masse and settled in, awaiting their bishop to begin his sermon. After a moment, the deep voice continued.

"Peace to you, my sisters and brothers. Today, let us examine this important question: What is luck and where does it come from? Why do some people seem to have so much luck and some don't seem to have any luck at all? The answer, of course, is quite simple. As the poets and the tablets and the sages and the stones of our religion have taught us since time immemorial, one's luck in this world is tied directly to their relationship with 7. The closer one lives to the number and its theurgy, the more righteous one becomes, the better one honors the goddesses and gods, and the greater the favor that shines down upon them.

"Naturally, the number 7 shows up all over the temple teachings: there's the cautionary tale of Andveek and the 7th sister, the story of Chara's 7 needles, the demigod parables of Syncho and Diasco, and of course the story of Pediós the Smoke Fox, to name a few. But the seminal tale of 7, the origin story of the temple's catechism, is found in the teachings we call, "Skopia's Numerology." And it's to these lessons that I want to turn today.

"Before we jump in on her mysticism, however, let's first revisit Skopia's mythology. You'll remember that Skopia was hatched from 1 of the 4 glass eggs laid by Sirzy- the Goddess of Immortality. Sirzy was a Phoenix and the offspring of the source gods Was and Will- the progenitors of all things- the 1st Causers of history and time. Now before Sirzy laid her holy eggs, she received a Bird Omen in a dream- no small thing for an avian deity, especially for a Phoenix. The prophecy was delivered by Galatia- the messenger goddess of Mythos- who told her that 1 of her 4 hatchlings would grow to become the Goddess of Life, thus threatening Sirzy's sovereignty over the human soul. Sirzy wasn't about to let that happen, so 3 days after the glass eggs hatched, she pushed the 4 godlings out of her nest- ostensibly to their deaths. Problem solved.

"But what Sirzy didn't account for was that 1 of the newborn beings, Skopia, would survive the fall and escape, assuming the form of a mountain goat and ascending to the hermitage atop Mount Sinopah. It's there Skopia was taken in by the monks of the place and cloaked as a novice, in order to hide her from Sirzy- who never stopped hunting the fugitive goddess.

"While secreted away in her sanctum, Skopia was taught the ways of the Sinopah monks, and spent the next 3½ centuries studying their habits and teachings, including their nascent understanding of the connection between the gods and numbers. Skopia became such a master of these teachings, that the holy order implored her to chronicle her lessons in scripture. That scripture is of course the *Seventicon*, the most important teaching of the High Temple. Which brings us back to our original point of consideration: Skopia's numerology and its underlying lessons of luck.

"*Seventicon* explains Skopia's divinity through a series of meditations on the topic of good fortune. In fact, many scholars regard *Seventicon* as the authoritative writ for understanding the magic of 7. And arguably the most significant and oft-quoted passage of our entire faith can be found in *Seventicon*'s '7th Meditation on Luck.' It reads:

> *If you seek the favor of the gods- that is, if you wish to maximize your luck in this life- remember that everything good derives from the holy number 7. So look for 7 all around; like the gods' benevolence- it's everywhere. Are you married? Do you have 3 kids, a couple of pets, maybe a brother? That's 1+3+2+1, and that equals 7. Your family is strong with divine favor. Were you born on the 18th? 1 from 8 is 7. Yours was a felicitous birth. How many letters in your name? How many birds are in that tree? How many steps on that ladder? Patterns of 7 are all around, and every one of them means blessing for you.*
>
> *It is not enough, however, simply to seek patterns of 7 in your life. Seeing them is but the 1st step. It is next incumbent on you to divine the meaning of these patterns. Why is 7 showing up in your life in the ways that it is? Who can answer this question better than you? You are the high priest of your own life, so you must decipher your own riddles. Do not fear misinterpreting the message; the gods will speak to you through intuition, and intuition will steer you to the truth.*
>
> *And don't ignore coincidence, either. There's no such thing. Coincidence is a game played by the gods to see if you're paying attention. If there is any synchronicity in your life, examine it. Look for meaning in every fortuity- it's there.*
>
> *And all of this is what it is. So let it be."*

"Let it be," responded the crowd mechanically. "And there you have it," continued the voice, "the most revered mandate of our faith, as delivered by the Goddess Skopia in her 7th meditation.

"In essence, Skopia gives us 3 directives: (1) seek 7 and its patterns in everything; (2) decipher the meaning of 7 in your life; and, (3) scrutinize synchronicity. Sounds straightforward, doesn't it? But how do we do it? How do we bring these seemingly simple rules to our everyday lives?

"Here is a good place to begin: anywhere you see a number in your life, examine it. Multiply it, add it, divide it, subtract it- do whatever you must do to get that number to 7. And once you have found your 7, then ask yourself where in your life does this 7 exist, because that is where your luck resides. And everywhere you find a 7, you will find luck. Then once you have found that luck, find more luck, and keep finding luck. And never stop looking for 7, because you will never stop finding luck if you look. And this goes on forever- seeking 7 and finding luck. And this is The Way, my sisters and brothers. So let it be."

At this, the recording abruptly ended and the chip reset. Then after checking the time, I put the player, the chip, and the stone back into their shoebox, tapped my pipe, brushed my teeth, and went to bed.

That night I dreamt a strange dream. I was in a nondescript location at an indeterminate time of day, sitting next to a man I could not see, but somehow knew to be my grandfather. He spoke: "How did you like the sermon?" he asked. His voice was honey and gold. I answered him honestly, "It seems like a good way to see meaning where there isn't any." After a thoughtful pause, "Skepticism always precedes Faith," he replied peacefully. And that's all I remember; then I awoke.

****

I'd never been devout, and though I did have my 7 Ceremony in the temple when I was 18, the decision was really more a nod to my grandpa's theistic heritage, than any expression of religious devotion on my part. I lived what you'd call a 'spiritual' but not 'religious' life. Unlike so many, I spent very little time thinking about my relationship to the goddesses and gods. As evidence, I hadn't seen the inside of a temple in over 15 years.

So I surprised myself when, some weeks after my birthday, I acknowledged that the sermon and its message had stuck with me. Also surprising, I started to experiment with 7. I found myself playing with numbers anytime I encountered one. If I was out at dinner, for example, I'd count the number of items on the menu, then subtract by the number of people sitting at the bar, then divide by the number of shoes I was wearing, et cetera, until I got to 7. Sometimes 7 would be easy to find ('Hey look- 7 coats on that rack!') and sometimes it took some manipulation to get there ('Hey look- if you subtract, divide, add, divide again, it's 7!'). But regardless of how I found it, it became increasingly apparent to me that one thing always remained consistent: it felt good to find 7.

In addition to looking for 7, I also went on the look for coincidence in my life, per Skopia's instruction. This proved the tougher task. Don't you find that when your attention is heightened to a thing, you start seeing that thing all over the place? Well, the same thing happened to me when I started looking for synchronicities- they were everywhere, and all of them were ripe with portent. Every animal was an omen, every redhead was a messenger of mystical import, each 'hello' I received was riddled with divine meaning. And when everything is a coincidence, you realize quite quickly that nothing is a coincidence.

But there was one coincidence that I just couldn't shake; I guess because it seemed more significant to me than the others. It was the connection between listening to my grandpa's sermon and then meeting him in a dream later that same night. And even this I tried to explain away, telling myself: "Of course I dreamt him that night- he was fresh in my mind, as was his sermon. What else could I be expected to dream about? It was no coincidence, no synchronicity..." But just on the heels of this sensible voice always came another. It was the honey and gold voice of my grandpa, and it would say in a tone so rich with peace it sounded like a song: "Skepticism always precedes Faith."

As time went on, I continued to look for 7 and its meaning in everything and everywhere. And I kept finding it, too. It got to where I was seeking 7 without even thinking about it; I was just going about my day, subconsciously registering 7s all around me: ("Passed 2 people in the hall, ate 1 sandwich for lunch, 4 red transports in the parking bay: 7. My day is charmed...") (Picked up Jack's call on the 3rd ring, 'Jack' has

4 letters: 7. Jack is a Mythos-sent friend...") (Cecily the barista smiled at me. My coffee cost 7.16 units: 7 and 1+6 equals double 7s. I should ask her out...") You get the point. And as 7-hunting became 2nd nature to me, 2 curious things started to happen.

1st of all, for real and for true, my luck actually started to improve. I started to always get the parking spot, always get the best seat, always get the biggest piece- things were going my way. But in other, more significant ways I felt my luck shifting, too. Like my life was focused- I was finally focused- on what mattered most. Everything was just... better, all around. I don't know how to explain it. And weirdly, it felt to me like it all had something to do with 7.

2ndly, although I couldn't deny this connection I was feeling to 7 and the luck that accompanied, I also couldn't explain it; and this was a growing problem for me. The main reason I originally turned from the temple is the impossibility of it all. Glass eggs and prophecies and magic: faith requires too much suspension of belief; it asks too much of me. Logic, on the other hand, feels comfortable. Facts and knowledge are much easier for me to get my head around than wisdom and paradox, so that's where I've always resided. But now I was faced with a truth that didn't stand to reason- the luck of 7- and it made me start to question the hegemony of logic.

Then in the midst of all this thinking and doubting, I had a day like no other- my cup overflowed. 7 was everywhere- and I mean everywhere: 7s from the newscasters on the teleview, 7s on the road to work, 7s in the break room, pub hour 7s with friends. I even found a 7 that night in my dinner. It was a happy, lucky, 7-filled day, and that night I went to bed as a man content with his place in the universe. I went to bed as a man rich with 7.

And as I slept and leapt in 7s that night, I met my grandfather in a 2nd dream.

This time we sat across from each other in a crowded space- maybe a cafe or restaurant. Grandpa was wearing a buffalo hide cassock and a turquoise-adorned miter, what I recognized to be the vestments reserved for the temple's 3 most sacred events: birthings, funerals, and 7 ceremonies. As happens in some dreams, time was distorted.

It felt like we'd been sitting together for a long while, though I can't say why. Our exchange was metered and calm, but there was chaos all around us- anger, argument, violence. Shots and screams rang in the distance; flames and fighting raged outside beyond the windows, but we were undaunted. I even sipped tea. "Been seeing some 7s lately, eh?" my grandpa asked calmly amidst the mayhem, "starting to make you think some weird stuff, huh?" "Yeah, about that," I replied (across the way a child screamed, a woman wailed), "why does this all seem... true? All the luck and the 7 stuff, it feels like it's working. How can that be?" My grandpa smiled serenely at this (an explosion rumbled through the distance) with a look of perfect tranquility in his eyes, and he spoke:

"When you exit this dream, you won't remember much, but I want you to try hard to remember this: Everything we think we know about what we believe, is wrong. And yet, everything we see, hear, and feel: the stories, the blessings, the 7s, all of it- is real, just not in the way we think. And it's all of it what it is, Son. We just gotta let it be."

And that's all I remember; then I awoke.

****

Mountain Shadows, Room 114
Paradise Valley, AZ
11/2021

give Spring away

...it's always the carrots that first give Spring away- **she thinks, standing at the sink and near the kitchen window***- and artichokes and apricots and... figs? I think maybe figs, too- fingers in, rock the blade back and forth, back and forth- remember to save the tips and ends for stock- and what is it anyway- just money- nothing but money- it's not the most important thing- back and forth- what's the most important thing? Family, that's the most important thing- and money, money's important too because it lets you do things- yes, but without family, what would you do?- "***Mom!" (from the other room)***- maybe he just forgot- forgot to tell you about the money? don't be naive- no, just, I don't know- how's that rice coming?- 10 more minutes, don't lift the lid-* **"Mom!" (closer now)** *what is it he thinks, that I'm too stupid to find out?- back and forth- is that what he thinks, that I don't pay attention to things, to things like money and- back and forth- and blonde hairs- ...and blonde hairs!- back and forth- the bastard!- last carrot- back and forth- where's that onion? dang it, forgot the onion-* **"Mooooom! What's for dinner?"** *-that's ok, don't need an onion- back and forth- blond hairs- and the money, I guess it wasn't that much money, but it's still money and we need money- back and forth- always need money- there, last carrot, ok into the pot-* **"Mom! (same room) I've been calling you- why haven't you answered me? What's for dinner?" "I heard you just fine. We don't yell across rooms to each other in this house. We're having chicken for dinner. It'll be ready in half an hour- go tell your brother."** *where was I now?*

****

blunt-knived mams

A general affront to his epicurean sensibilities, slow-cooker cooking is the lazy refuge of blunt-knived mams- or so he thought prior to tasting this admixture of exotic sensory delight. The marriage of color and texture, the warm-spiced smell, the unctuous-yet-chewy-graveled mouth feel, not to mention the explosion of flavor; never in his life has Jimmy Thibideaux tasted anything so sublime as the crock-served amuse-gueule upon which he now unrestrainedly sets himself. "Who made this?" he purrs quietly to Carol, as he grabs yet another baguette slice and dunks it greedily into the bubbling pot- not even caring that he's in up past the first knuckle. "I did," she perks happily, enjoying Jimmy's enjoyment. "I call it, 'Carol's Queso.' It's a family favorite. I usually make it with sausage, but this time I used ground elk. Hank pulled a tag last season." Jimmy stuffs in the entire cheese-slopped slice then says before chewing, "It's amazing! Not too spicy- just right." "I'll get you the recipe. I like to experiment with heat. Sometimes I use jalapenos. This time I tried..."

Next to Jimmy and Carol, half-listening but not participating, stands Dexter Ambrose, Adolescent Toxicity Claims Associate and 2-year cubicle-mate of Tammy Lafont: Metatex Customer Complaints Division woman-of-the-hour. Having had a large breakfast, Dexter- despite the enticing pot luck laid out before him- limits his noshing to a deviled egg, a few carrot sticks, a peanut butter brownie, and two snickerdoodles. Overhearing Carol's dip so enthusiastically panegyrized, he also resolves to try the queso, as soon as finger-licking Jimmy gets out of the way. Competing for Dexter's attention with Carol's soliloquy on the merits of roasted versus unroasted Hatch chiles is the memory of a long-ago conversation he and Tammy once had over the top of their cubicle divider.

One of the charms of sharing intimate work space with another is that you get to hear half of all the details of their calls, when not on one of your own. Tammy was coming off an animated exchange with a caller who was wrapped around the axle about a cancer diagnosis and its presumed connection to the cadmium content of the recently-recalled Metatex ZR-4000 Hyperlight Thoughtdrive. As the company's first line of defense, Tammy's job is to take the call, log the complaint, and forward the details to Tort Prevention- a sizable department housed off-campus a few miles away in the Metatex east annex near Liversburg. If you can detach yourself from the calls and don't mind getting yelled at, it's an easy job. Tammy can and doesn't, and so for her- it is.

"Jill has put me in a tight spot," Dexter remembers Tammy saying as she popped her head over the divider like a gopher, picking up the thread of their conversation from an hour ago; her cancer call entirely forgotten as soon as the particulars were keyed in and the connection cut. "She wants me to keep quiet about a thing, and I'm not sure I should." Dexter knew that response was neither expected nor required so he held his tongue, and after a quick glance around the office bay to ensure no one was listening, she continued. "Apparently, Jill's mom has come down with a touch of the chlamydia." She dramatically lowers her voice at the word 'chlamydia' and Dexter inwardly stifles a giggle, but his visage reveals nothing. Tammy continues... "She got divorced a while back and has been dating a bit. A bit too much, it sounds like to me." (friendly silence from Dexter) "Of course Jill is horrified and doesn't want anyone to know, but I just don't think a thing like that can be kept a secret. It's none of my business what Jill's mom does- and of course I'm not going to say anything to anyone, but now she's putting out germs to unsuspecting others, and I don't think that's right. If the word gets out, she has no one to blame but herself. Like I always say, you reek what you show." (more smiling silence from Dexter) "Karma always wins in the end. That's another thing I say..."

As Dexter reminisces on the unfortunate lot of Jill's mom, all the while inching closer to the purling vat of Carol's Queso, across the room Victor Ramirez, Metatex Vice President of Malfeasance and Resolution, is eulogizing soon-to-be-retiring Tammy: who stands beaming by his side- alternately blushing and nodding at Vic's flatteries- and laughing in all the right places. His hand rests lightly on her shoulder.

"...One of the keys to doing this job well is keeping and using your head when things get hot, and nobody does it better than Tammy here," Victor is saying. His hand moves to her forearm. "I remember happening by her pod one day when she was fielding a particularly nasty call. Had to do with a kid having its eye put out. I think it was blunt trauma from a first-gen Virtual Immersion Helmet. Some of you here remember the headaches those things gave us." (laugh-groans from around the room) "It was actually a laser injury from the helmet's high-res visor, Vic," Tammy corrects. "Oh yeah, that's right. Anyhow, the call went south fast and had real Level 5 potential, but Tammy stayed cool. Without giving anything away, she quietly live-loops one of the Tort Prev guys, then flips her Auto-Scripter to manual and lets the lawyer drive. With his help, Tammy steers the conversation around to an admission that the user instructions were received by audio playback off a handheld and not uploaded to a local hard drive, per the disclaimer. Tammy even got the mother to admit that when the kid got hurt, in her rush to get to the hospital, she didn't properly power down the unit before she left the house. The whole thing was recorded and gave the Litigation Team enough daylight to settle quickly and prevent a full-blown product malfunction case. It was beautiful. (playful cheers, claps and even a joking 'huzzah' pop up around the room) And that's just one example. In 20 years of service, she's got a million of them. No one is going to miss you more than me, Tam- thanks for everything." He is now holding her hand in both of his, her eyes are soft. Despite the subtle drama unfolding between Vic and Tam, few of the Metatex Family are absorbing the nuance, as their attention has just been elsewhere drawn.

It is a nearly-universal truth: spend enough time in the corporate bowels and eventually you too will be seduced by the company cake. The Company Cake: the primary, and oftentimes only reason anyone shows up to these things. It's the lure that brings them in, it's the promise that makes them stay. For everyone knows, the cake isn't cut until the speeches are made, the crocodile tears shed, and the plaques dispensed. Then out it comes in all its glory, to be sliced and apportioned to those with stamina enough to outlast the blather.

But don't be fooled. For unlike company employees everywhere, all company cakes are not created equal (for more on how everyone is the same but different, see the HR Handbook, page 13, "Core Values,

Mission Statement, and Active Shooter Protocol"). To those uninitiated, it might surprise you to know that the secret to a superior company cake is not in the cake. Sure, some cakes are moister than others, some people prefer chocolate to vanilla, some are occasionally put off by a nut allergy, but these are hair-splitting distractions that take one's eye off the ball from the real deal maker: the frosting.

There are many types of frosting, each with its attendant votary. Some prefer ganache, some royal icing, some stiff-peaked meringue. Some others' favorite is buttercream, or whipped cream, even. A simple glaze is the choice of yet others still. For Marjorie Mayfield, however, nothing but cream cheese frosting will do. Something about the simple combination of butter, vanilla, powdered sugar, and farmer cheese just really floats her boat. And here it comes now, rolling out on a gurney big enough to carry a cadaver, replete with sparkler candles and serenaded by a rousing version of, "For She's a Jolly Good Fellow," led by none other than division heavyweight and office Lothario, Victor Ramirez.

It's a gorgeous gateau, for which no expense was spared. Multi-tiered and flower-strewn, oozing with decadence and covered, of course, in cream cheese frosting. So why the look of concern, Marjorie? Is it because you're afraid you won't get a slice? Nothing to fear there- that cake is big enough to feed this room of 150 twice over. Is it because you're going to miss Tammy and her Monday morning humble-brags? ("...Phil and I took the boys out on the boat this weekend. For such a small thing, it sure does go fast...") Hardly; you don't even know Tammy. Maybe it's because you don't belong here. Maybe it's because you snuck into the building under the guise of a family-friend-congratulations-Tammy-well-wisher. Maybe it's because you're afraid someone will peel back your subterfuge and check your pockets. Is that it, Marjorie- are you afraid they'll find what's in your pocket? No bandwidth for doubt now: cake time is go time...

Boardroom rules of engagement have taken a dark turn since the slog back from the most recent Depression. In fairness, the crater caused by the last impact took grit to crawl out of. We blew it deep. And where bloody knuckles and a strong chin were enough before to fight your way over and through the gold-backed jungle, this time you'd better have a blade in your hind pocket if you want a piece. Or better yet, a gun. For while the most successful corporate leaders of this New Economy necessarily espouse "Of The People" principles, their egalitarian veneer encases the heart, mind, and soul of the timeless totalitarian. With one hand the people must be deftly-led. Loose hand on the reins, so to speak. "Don't mind me in the saddle, it's you choosing our course..." In the other hand- behind the back- is the cat 'o nine tails- hidden from view, but ready for lashing. Discretion is required to know when to use which, and hair trigger resolve is key once the choice is made. It's a subtle balance to maintain; too nerve wracking for the faint-of-heart, and ill-suited to the merely brutal. As in all such regimes, paranoia runs rampant. Ever-present in the minds of those at the table's head is the question: how do I keep my seat? Ever-present in the minds of those around the table: how do I get to the head? In both cases, the answer is insidious in its simplicity: by any means necessary.

All regenerative systems require new modalities to survive. Evolve or cease to exist: it's an unavoidable binary. Nowhere is this principle more starkly on display than in the realm of biological heritability. But evolution is a two-pronged fork. Sometimes the more direct route to progress is not waiting for fins to form feet, but rather to kill and eat your rival. Business is the same.

It's in this spirit of eating one's rivals that Darkguard was formed. Known as a *night label outfit,* it's not a name you'll find in any respectable business directory, though their closely-guarded client list is meters long and spans the globe. Their skill set is broad and their services bespoke, but throughout every contract weaves a similar thread: Assassination. That's not to say they're murderers for hire (though anything for a price). No, their services typically offer a more delicate tracery. Violence of the Darkguard variety favors focus on the target's virtue, not their person. This was not always the case. In the early days of the firm's inception, many a St. Moritz ski accident or Gulfstream malfunction could be traced back via complex trajectory to a Darkguard operative. But over time it was discovered that fewer questions were asked, fewer eyebrows raised when the target in question met their end not by some suspicious violence, but by a revealed turpitude of the victim's own making. Fewer tears are always shed for the pedophile than for the playboy. And so the service offering of "character assassination" rose to the top of the Darkguard menu.

At first blush it might seem surprising, shocking even, to know how quickly the queue filled with aspirant Darkguard patrons. Hundreds, thousands from around the business globe took a number and stood in line waiting for their chance to take the legs out from under their respective challengers. As heads rolled and rumors flowed, Darkguard's name was increasingly whispered on squash courts and back nines from New York to Tokyo, and everywhere in between. For the well-appointed executive, it became de rigueur to have "ACME" -the alias for Darkguard's international answering service- included in one's contact list.

In a stroke of marketing genius, the firm eventually began promoting its services to the business world's echelon of middle management. And that's when the iron got real hot. It turns out that many executives eventually assume a level of professional exhaustion in their lives. They have most of what they want and can no longer muster the same bloodlust needed to heed that animal call to kill or be killed. Not so the Middle Manager. For there is perhaps no thirst greater than that of Branch Manager Bob wanting to become Senior Vice President Robert. And there are many Bobs out there who will do anything to slake that thirst.

It's a subtle art, that of discreditation. One can't simply hang flyers around town saying, "Tom Smith beats his wife," or, "Sally Jones embezzles." Such ham handed tactics will engender naughty no-no finger wagging and heads shaken in indignant disapproval, but the damage inflicted will be glancing at best. To really wreak havoc one doesn't throw stones, one plants seeds; seeds that in time rot to dead gardens of opprobrium. The requisite tools in the kit are myriad and must be employed with patience and precision. Forgery is a cornerstone: rentals, purchases, deposits, withdrawals; all manner of electronic movement must be falsified. This includes the movement of data: files and photographs, most specifically. Historical records must be doctored: educational, medical, criminal, financial. And all must conform to the same storyline: "Ms. or Mr. X does bad things when no one is looking. They're not who you think they are."

It's not just placement of data that must be attended to, however. Covering one's tracks is equally critical in this age of digital forensics. Every byte must be intentionally placed and accounted for, lest the discreditor be discredited and the mark made a martyr. Every. Single.

Byte. It's a resource-heavy enterprise, Darkguard, employing many of the world's most-gifted coders, hackers, programmers, and digital sharpshooters: a team of geniuses to rival any company in the world. But the crème de la crème of Darkguard's impressive stable is not to be found in the labyrinthine corridors of its undisclosed location, but on the frontlines of the world's business battlefield. For the company's truest shadow walkers- its ninjas- are the Droppers.

Digital evidence is condemning, and many a competitor of the wrong person has been marched before the corporate and social firing squad via the path of counterfeit files and sham communiqués, but the true coup de grâce- that finishing round to the back of the head- is always best-delivered by physical, tactile proof. Crumpled polaroids, lipstick-smudged collars, errant ATM receipts: these are the fate-sealers of the Unwitting Damned. And while hacking into a target's system and implanting untraceable data from hundreds or even thousands of kilometers away requires an expertise only a handful of people in this world possess, breaking into that same person's home or office- their physical space- and executing an undetected plant requires an operative with the guile and stealth of a serpent. It requires a Dropper. A Dropper like Marjorie.

If you can crash one effectively, parties are a great time to drop. No one ever really knows everyone, and you can claim confusion if caught wandering. All the better if there are drunks and drugs- keeps the revelers foggy. Daytime office parties- like this one- are generally dry, but there's always a window when the crowd's regard is collectively absorbed. Cake time is go time.

Personally, Marjorie (not her real name) cares nothing about the mark, it's just a file number to her. Professionally, however, Marjorie cares very much about the details, and knows nearly everything there is to know about Yumi Tan, President of the Metatex Media Steerage Division. Marjorie's Yumi file includes such specifics as her family background, her finances, her proclivities, her aversions, her medical history, her spending habits, her social habits, and her eating habits- to name a few. It also includes the names, locations and specifics of her family and friends, as well as her known enemies- one of whom evidently has a big ax to grind. Conventional wisdom suggests the more complete the file, the more refined the drop.

Present directive calls for two puts, the first of which was made in the parking garage on the way into the party. In the far back of Yumi's glove box (plate number BR3G-26L5), surreptitiously tucked by Marjorie beneath the vehicle registration, owner's manual, proof of insurance, and a pouch of sanitizing wipes, is a neatly folded and innocuous-looking receipt from a very specific car wash, performed on a very specific date, and paid for with a very specific credit card. When discovered, and hopefully no time soon, the receipt and its implications will have all the nuance of a knowing glance, and carry with it all the force of a slug to the chest.

Based on previously purloined floor plans, Marjorie knows that Yumi's office is on the building's ground floor, one deck below the party. Workhorse Yumi spends 12-14 hours a day locked away in her office, so a desk drawer or sofa cushion plant was deemed unfeasible, as was a purse plant- which is possible, but unnecessarily risky in this case. Consequently, the first floor employee break room was chosen as the location of the second put; more specifically, the back of the pantry's top shelf. It's there, with gloved hands, that Marjorie now quickly but deliberately places a zip-sealed bag containing three homemade cookies- Grandma Tan's recipe- across the front of which is written: "Yumi's- don't eat." One of the three cookies has been adulterated with a very incriminating trace of synthetic necrotoxin DN-1218: an experimental compound, the only extant sample of which recently disappeared from the heavily-guarded R&D facility of Mundo Farmacéutica in Madrid. Similar to the receipt, the hope and intention is for it to take some time for this breadcrumb to be discovered. As call center maven and weekend boating enthusiast Tammy LaFont might say, "Revenge is a fish best served old."

A job isn't done until final extraction, and sound procedure dictates one move swiftly but casually from the drop site to pre-arranged transport, as quickly as possible. Marjorie has scouted several departure routes, the most expedient of which is the building's main ingress/egress just out and to the left of the break room door. It leads straight across the parking lot to the public bus stop- where the 1:15 will be along any minute. She moves toward it now, then pauses in recollection. "I really shouldn't," she thinks aloud, then glances at her watch. "But there's always the 1:25. What the hell..."

Then out the break room and hard right, Marjorie heads for the elevator and up to the second floor, where she rejoins the party just in time to have a taste of that cream cheese frosting atop a slice of the company cake.

****

fairy tales, four

Once upon a time there was a kind and aging king who had a cruel and selfish son. The king was much-vexed because he sensed the time approaching when he would be called home to the realm of his forefathers. He knew when he sailed that distant shore, his crown would pass to one unfit to rule, thus plunging his kingdom to ruin and his subjects to despair.

So the king announced a trial to find the wisest and most valiant of his land. The first to answer three questions to the king's satisfaction would inherit the throne and rule his enchanted kingdom. Answering them not to the king's pleasure meant banishment to the wilderness and death by beasts and cold. So as not to arouse his son's suspicion, the prince and those counselors loyal to him were sent by the king on an errand of royal business to a far away land.

One day, an unlikely young girl arrived at the castle's gate, seeking audience with the king. She was thirteen harvests aged, grown fifteen hands high, and had honest eyes of hazel flecked with spots of gold. Her chestnut curls were rope-thick and woven with a fragrant garland of wildflowers and woodland herbs. She wore the threadbare frock of a farm girl and walked on shoeless feet. Upon her shoulder sat a magpie and by her side walked a small-horned and white-eared goat. She held no leash as none was needed- the goat went as she went and never left her side. The magpie fed on pumpkin seeds from a pocket on her dress, and she whispered time to time in its feathered ear. It seemed to whisper back. "You seek the crown, Child?" queried the king. "I seek a peaceful realm, My Lord," her mild reply. "So listen well and answer me this question first of three." Then spake he thus the following tale...

Once upon a time there was a shepherd boy who lived with his father in the foothills and tended their flock of sheep in the mountain meadows above. It was lonely in the alpine heights and the boy's only plaything was a silver ball that he always had near and loved with all his heart.

One day the ball rolled off a ledge and under a large stone, out of the boy's reach. He was much lamented and sat on the ground to weep. A snake slithered by and said to the child, "Why do you weep, Boy?" "I've lost my favorite plaything under that stone, and I fear I shall never have it back. It's my only friend in this lonely place." "Have heart," the snake replied, "...I am slight and can slide under the stone to get your ball. I will do this for you if you promise to be my friend- for I too am alone and lonely here." The boy agreed and the snake retrieved the toy. Both were joy filled: the boy to have his plaything, the snake to have a friend.

Later that night as the boy and his ball nestled into his shepherd's hut, the snake slid in and curled at the boy's feet. "What are you doing?" said the boy. "We are friends now and I want to share your hut. It is cold in the cave where I live." "Go from here- this is no place for a snake," replied the boy. And the saddened snake slithered away.

The next morning the boy and his sheep left the high meadow and headed down to the foothills, for the grazing season was done and it was almost time to take the fattened flock to market. Nestled once again in his father's hearth-warmed cottage, the boy with his ball fell to restful sleep. He was woken before dawn, however, by a soft hiss in his ear- again it was the snake.

"Why did you leave me in the mountains, Boy? That is no way to treat a friend." The boy in fear and anger grabbed the snake by its tail and flung it into the night. "Go from here, snake, and don't come back. Beasts and boys aren't meant as friends." Heartbroken, the snake slid away. But as it left, it bit the heel of three ewes and three lambs each- sending them all to death. Then the snake returned to its high-up cave, its trust in man forever shattered.

When the boy's father awoke before the sun and found his six sheep dead, he flew into a rage and beat his shepherd son. Then he made the boy sell his silver ball at market to pay for the animals he'd lost. The boy wept bitterly for his misfortune and everafter killed every snake he saw. So goes the tale of, 'The Serpent and the Toy.'

His story complete, the king looked to the girl and asked, "Tell me, Little One, was the serpent just in its killing of the sheep?" With a steady stare and little pause, the girl replied, "Alas, My Liege, 'twas not. It was the serpent's will to trust, and the boy's will to betray. So too did the serpent choose its path when it took the road of revenge. My parents- may Heaven keep them both- taught me vengeance is a venom most harmful to the doer, not the done-to. And so My Lord I must say the serpent was wrong in its reprisal."

With inscrutable gaze, the king delayed for a moment stroking his beard, engrossed in regal thought. Then with a satisfied nod he spoke, "Verily, Child, your words ring wise and true. So hear what's next and answer my question two..."

Once upon a time there were two unlikely friends named Wave and Flame. They were born of separate tribes, each camp forsworn to war with the other. Despite the raging feud between their clans, the two decided to live together in fraternal peace, and established a common house.

The friends set aside shared gold to buy winter provisions, so when icy storms arrived, they would have food and warmth for the season. They placed ten coins in a pouch of hide and buried it in the woods. "When winter comes we shall dig up the gold and be happy that we have it," said each to the other.

One day at market Wave saw a silver hammer he greatly wished to have, though he had no money to buy it. He snuck to the woods and took two coins from the hide pouch, then bought the hammer and took it home. "Where did you get that fine hammer?" asked Flame when he saw it. "A gift from a grateful nobleman whose child I saved from drowning," answered Wave. And Flame raised a toast to his friend's courageous deed.

Not long after, Wave was back at market and spied a saddle of excellent craft and filigree. He snuck again to the forest and took coins from the buried pouch to buy it, then saddled his swaybacked donkey and rode home feeling dandy and proud. "Where did you get that fine saddle, Wave?" asked Flame, for he knew his friend had not the money to buy it. "A gift from a grateful nobleman whose wife I saved from drowning," answered Wave. And Flame raised a toast to his twice-courageous friend, though doubt whispered in his ear.

Autumn approached and Wave was once again at market. This time a fanciful hourglass caught his eye. "What a fine thing it would be to have that on my mantel," thought Wave, though of course he had not the money to buy it. So he snuck to the woods and took the last of the coins from the hide pouch, then brought home his new and shiny knickknack.

"Where did you get that hourglass?" asked Flame, as Wave proudly placed the bauble on their worn and humble table. "A gift from a grateful nobleman whose horse I saved from drowning," answered Wave. This time Flame was greatly suspicious and though he said nothing, nor did he toast his friend's courage, but sat rather in uncertain silence.

Then the north wind blew down upon them, and it was time to provision for winter. When Flame retrieved the hide pouch from the wood and found it empty, he knew at once that Wave had taken their gold and squandered it. He flew to anger and spoke harshly to Wave. "You have wasted our gold on selfish conceit!" he raged. "Do not speak to me like this," warned Wave, for his arrogance would not allow him to admit his folly. "It will be a cold and hungry winter because of you, Proud Fool!" bellowed Flame.

Wave did not like to be yelled at and flew into a rage of his own. He took the silver hammer and smashed his friend's skull, killing him to silence. So guilt-ridden was he by this hateful deed that Wave then flung himself to the sea, where he died most horribly in the jaws of an ocean beast. So goes the tale of, 'The Pouch of Hidden Hide.'

"Tell me, Child," spoke the king after a quiet pause, "who's vanity led this pair to ruin?" "May it please My Lord," spoke the girl after a pause of her own, "the fault was equal-shared. For having thrown their family quarrel to disregard and chosen a home forbidden by their fathers, their ruin was rightly-received." The king again stroked his beard (a habit he had when thinking deeply) and then replied, "But Child," he spoke, "wasn't it noble and good for these two friends to seek accord where their families had failed? Must not it be the fate of some pioneer to take the plunge for peace, despite possible pain unto them?"

At this the magpie on the girl's shoulder leaned close its beak into her ear, and though no sound could be heard by any but she, the girl nodded softly, then lifted her eyes to the king and spoke. "My Lord, forgive me. More distant sees your learned gaze than mine. Peace before pride is ever the nobler aim." At these words the king was well-pleased, for to hear with an open heart sound suggestion from worthy counsel is the hallmark of prudence and wisdom. "I am happied by thee," returned the king, "so hear once more and answer this, the last of my questions three."

Once upon a time there lived a widowed huntsman and his baby girl deep in an ancient wood. One day the huntsman came upon a falcon with an injured wing, lying still near a brook. The huntsman mended the falcon's wing and placed it in a tree where it would be safe until it could heal and return to the sky. As the huntsman turned to go, there was a flash of brilliant light and the falcon revealed itself to be a beautiful sorceress.

"You have saved me, Huntsman," spoke the enchantress, "and so I grant you a wish in return for your kindness." The huntsman was a humble man and had no want of wealth or power. He asked instead that the sorceress take his young daughter and teach her in the ways of good magic. "This wish I grant you," spoke the kind witch, and she brought the girl to her enchanted garden, where she raised her as her own. There the girl learned to cast charms and spells and to draw magic from the woods. She befriended the flowers and the woodland creatures and was known by them as a kind and gentle spirit.

One day, when the girl had grown to the age of sixteen, the enchantress- having business afar- entreated the girl to tend the magic garden while she was away. The good witch took the girl by the hand and led her to a part of the garden she had never seen before, where there stood a tall stone wall with three doors embedded: one of iron, one of gold, and one of silver. The enchantress told the girl that while she could enter the doors of iron and gold, she must not touch the door of silver. The girl told her mistress she would obey, and with that the enchantress turned to a falcon's form and flew from the garden, leaving the girl alone.

She was anxious to see what secrets the two doors held and the girl entered the iron door first. Within its chamber was revealed the truth of war and peace. The girl was filled with understanding of how to end the strife of all mankind, and her heart was greatly gladdened by this knowledge. She next entered the door of gold and therein were revealed the secrets of possession and worldly goods. She came to see how the evil of greed could be conquered, and poverty and dearth amongst all peoples relieved. In this knowledge her spirit grew light and hope abounded.

As she turned from the stone wall and went to leave the three doors for other parts of the garden, temptation gripped her and a voice within her crooned, 'Surely just a peek through the silver door won't hurt. My mistress is away and she'll never know if I tarry a moment longer.' At this the girl entered the forbidden door and terrible power and mystery consumed her. For within its chamber was revealed the nature and truth of all the universe- a knowledge too great for any worldborn creature to contain.

In a burst of light and flame, the girl was flung from the silver chamber and across the garden, where she lay- deaf, dumb, and blind- until the sorceress returned from her errand and found the girl in an unconscious heap. With a charm the good witch restored the girl's hearing, but not her voice or sight, and spoke to her thus, "You have disobeyed me, Child, and broken my trust. You are unworthy of the garden and must live once again amongst men and their treachery." At this, the enchantress cast the girl from her magic garden and left her in an empty wood.

For many years the girl wandered, unable to see or speak, surviving on what meager rations the forest dislodged. Until one day a young woodsman happened upon her, and though she was bedraggled and disarranged from years spent in blind and speechless wander, he could see she was beautiful and kind. He took her to his forest lodge where she found rest and recovered from her trial. After a time, the two married and had twin girls, whom they named Hope and Faith.

One night in a dream the girl was visited by the enchantress, who asked her to repent for seeking the silver door. 'You flung me to the forest and left me to die. But I was strong and found my own way to a happy life. I repent nothing, Evil Witch. Now leave me and don't return!' spoke the girl to her mistress. 'Your vanity grieves me,' replied the enchantress, and left the girl's dream, taking with her the baby Hope.

Though saddened by the loss of their child, the blind, mute wife and her woodsman groom lived on in the woods and cherished their daughter Faith. Some time passed and the girl was again visited in a dream by the enchantress, who once more entreated her to repent for seeking the silver door and its unbridled light. 'You abandoned me and took my Hope besides. I will never repent. Now go, Witch, and don't return!' spoke the girl with fervent rage. Saddened by the intense passion of the girl's pride, the enchantress left the dream and took with her this time the baby Faith.

When she awoke and found her second child gone, the girl gnashed her teeth in misery and beat her chest in anguish. She took herself to the wood's highest cliff in order to fling herself to death on the sharp-stoned vale below. As she stood on the rocky ledge- one step from her demise- she thought to empty heaven, 'Forgive me, Mistress, my vanity and pride! I sought the silver door in disobeyance of your command. You are just, and I am a fool!' As these thoughts crossed the girl's mind and she prepared to step to her wretched fate, thunder shook the sky and the enchantress appeared. The girl's sight and voice returned and she saw her mistress before her, holding in her arms the babies Hope and Faith. "Your humble truth restores you," spoke the kind witch, then changed to the form of a falcon and flew away, over the valley below, leaving the mother and her children to joyful reunion. So goes the tale of, 'The Door of Silver Secrets.'

"And now the final question," smiled the king, for he sensed he'd found his heir. "What power compelled the wise witch to have such patience with the girl- whose defiance and pride cost nearly all she held dear?"

"'Twas that magic that makes all the world work, My Lord," answered the girl without wait, "'twas Love that steered her mercied heart."

At this the king clapped his hands and rose from his throne in joyful triumph, for it was confirmed: his heir was found. At once he brought the girl- along with her goat and bird- to live in the castle, and he spent the rest of his days teaching her the ways of wise rule. When his time came, the king passed in contented peace, for he knew the crown went to one worthy of its weight.

After many moons, the king's son and his loyalists returned from their travels to find a new heir on the gone-king's throne. His father's trickery filled the prince with murderous fury, and he departed the kingdom enraged. He swore to return with an army and make war on the kingdom, putting the young queen's head on a stick, and retaking his rightful crown. A great and mighty battle ensued. But that is a different tale to be told another time...

****

yellow cars fade in the sun

He's been proving people right his whole life: "Debra Wonkowski will never go out with you, and if you keep lurking around her locker, you're going to come off looking like a creepy weirdo." Correct. "You should get white or sand, yellow cars fade in the sun." Correct. "You can't drink and eat your way to developing an immunity to lactose intolerance, that's not how it works." Extremely correct. But for some reason- call it hardheadedness, call it lack of self-awareness, call it vanilla-flavored bad decision making- despite having the benefit of reasonable counsel all around him, Toby Drebber just keeps listening to that slurred voice in his head. They aren't overly dramatic, his bad decisions. It's not like he shoots heroin into his eyeballs. There's just this barely-there vibe of 'oops' infused into everything he does: directions say 'left,' he goes right; he buys AA, the thing takes AAA; he only packs flip flops, it snows all weekend. So while nothing catastrophic ever happens, his life- by virtue of his perpetually questionable choices- has assumed a subtly downward trajectory. In childhood it wasn't that pronounced- all kids seem to be more-or-less playing on an even field. But now that he's 27, the gap between him and the pack has become noticeably wide. Problematic for the almost 30-year old who's banging around down here while his contemporaries are adulting up there, opportunities for meaningful engagement (professional, social, romantic, et cetera) are scant. Thank goodness for Skate Castle.

When he first saw it, pulling into the parking lot at Pete Gunther's 8th birthday party nearly 20 years ago, Toby was decidedly underwhelmed. It didn't look like a castle at all. It looked more like an enclosed steel and cinder block hay shed; there were no turrets, no battlements, and- unless you include the trash-choked irrigation ditch running along the property's east boundary- there wasn't even a moat. But once over its threshold and through the fortress's faux iron gates, that ill-impression flipped to its head. A squealing, giggling gallimaufry of childhood delights greeted him on the other side of the door. For it was on the inside where Skate Castle earned its stripes. Crests and swords adorned every booth along the back wall of "Lady Fairydust's Pizza Parapet." Tapestries chronicling the heroics of Sir Geoffry Joystick's many and lionhearted campaigns- including his slaying of the big purple dragon-festooned the ceiling above the skeeball, video game, and pinball machines of his eponymous arcade- just to the right of Lady Fairydust and just to the left of Ye Olde Skate Checkout and Return Counter. On every wall of this enchanted plaza were hand painted murals of bucolic, medieval scenes: knights and damsels, jesters and beasts, fairies and wizards galore, all of it serving to excite the collective imagination of the kingdom's visiting boys and girls. And encircled within it all was the main attraction: 20,000 square feet of light-flashing, music-pumping Royal Roller Rink. Countless opening acts of innocence have been played upon this stage: meaningful glances first met, shy seeking hands first held, and novice lips first kissed; not to mention the numerous breakings of young hearts and arms. A childhood Xanadu, it was Toby's inaugural lesson in the pitfalls of judging a book by its cover. Though dreary on the outside, on the inside, Skate Castle was literally the coolest thing he'd ever seen. And if Providence would but abide, Toby Drebber aspired to never, ever leave.

It's good fortune for most of us that Heaven largely ignores our supplications to grant childhood wishes. Were it not the case, there'd be at present many more astronaut cowboys, unicorn kitties, and ice cream truck drivers in population than there are surgeons and engineers; and one can be forgiven for thinking that not the best division of society's labor. But, Lo and Thunder! For 8-year-old Toby's petitions to Fate *were* heeded, and Skate Castle became his all-but-place-of domicile. It started with skates from Santa and an annual "Castle Pass" from Mom on his 9th Christmas. It didn't hurt that Mom- Kiki to her friends- preferred to spend what few hours she had away from duties as Assistant Manager of ladies' shoes at DeSilva's with her boyfriend, Chris. She actually encouraged Toby to spend as much time at the Castle as he liked- at least she knew where he was, and an annual pass was cheaper than babysitters. So Toby became a fixture. But despite his near daily visits and the well-earned designation of "rink rat" by fellow regulars, friends were few. Toby was a shy kid, and preferred to hide within the relative anonymity of the rink crowd, amidst the darkness and chaos of the oval, as opposed to the bright lights and social obligations of the snack bar and arcade. But he never begrudged the thousands of solitary laps he took around that parqueted floor. A lonesome afternoon of loops at Skate Castle was always preferable to the alternative: a self-warmed frozen dinner, TV, and the empty house at home. It wasn't loneliness, but the soul-grating silence of being alone that he sought to escape.

As the years rolled on- grade school to middle school, middle school to high school, high school to adulthood- Toby rolled round and round with them, and in time two advantages ensued. The first was that his skating improved dramatically. After a few years, he was by far the best in the arena, but more than that, the kid had skillz. Of course he developed mastery of the oldies: Hip Snatch, Boogie Curve, Soul Kick, Slant Slide, Latin Cross Wiggle, and so forth. But, as all masters do, Toby eventually ascended beyond tradition and into that rarified air of self-creation. He invented and named his own moves- feats of wheeled athleticism and daring-do that few were brave enough to attempt: Infinite Crossunder, Australian Cha-Cha, Kiki Cannonball, and of course, the gasp-inducing Tobias Top Drop- a twisting, back-flipping, somersaulting number that took its namesake daredevil years to master, and commanded as its wage more than a few sprained wrists and cracked foreheads along the way. As with all the greats, Toby- in his orbit- grew in reputation and acclaim and eventually began to acquire groupies. Unfortunately for under-gratified Toby, roller skating sycophants tend to be of the prepubescent variety, and so- outside the confines of Skate Castle- this did his 20-something social life little actual good. But at least there was a half acre of this planet where Toby was king and could revel in the warming glow of tween adulation. And that beat the incessant ribbing of now-stepdad Chris, and his constant reminders to Toby of his want for female companionship.

The second advantage of Toby's near-always Skate Castle hanging about, was that it eventually got him a job. At some point along the way, after the day's skating was done, Toby grabbed a broom and started helping Mr. Aquino clean up after closing. In time, the broom became a spatula as Toby rose into the role of Lady Fairydust Grillmaster. Next was a can of disinfectant as he was made Head Tuner at Ye Olde Skate Counter. The most recent advancement finds Toby wearing the plastic crown, clip-on tie, and personalized name tag of the Castle's most-coveted role and the palace's true seat of power: Skate Castle Royal Roller Rink Disk

Jockey, aka DJ Drebber. The promotion was in every way a surprise; DJ Merlin had been spinning tracks at Skate Castle since time immemorial. But some unforeseen misfortune had befallen him, as vaguely alluded to by Mr. Aquino when offering Toby the coveted keys to the Castle, and frankly, Toby was too dazed in the moment to ask clarifying questions. The long and the short of it was this: DJ Merlin was out, did DJ Drebber want in?

Having basically spent his entire childhood with the Skate Castle soundtrack playing in the background, Toby is well-studied on the heady responsibilities of the roller rink disk jockey, and his intuitions on when to employ the trade's various tools are consummate. Reverse Skate, Ladies' Choice, Lights-Low Lover's Loop: DJ Drebber always seems to know the right moment for all of it. And swirling infused through, under, over, and around everything is the playlist. His music bench is deep and his memory encyclopedic. In fact, so attuned is he to the emotional vicissitudes of his preteen subjects, that he is able to often retrieve and play that perfect song, at the perfect moment, to elicit the perfect response- before it's even asked for. Many a tear shed, many a fight averted, many an apology offered- one to the other- by hormone-fueled youths, too wrapped up in the emotion of the moment to realize that their words and actions were gently influenced- steered even- by the suggestive lyrics playing backdrop to their drama. DJ Drebber is such a maestro of the rink that he seems sometimes not to be playing music at all, but rather to be playing his audience- like an instrument; or better yet, conducting them- like an orchestra. Hamsters in his wheel, All; yes indeed, as concerns Skate Castle: Tobias Drebber is Master.

A timeworn truth to which DJ Drebber can attest: rank has its privileges. Skates at cost, unlimited Lady Fairydust refills, twenty credits per day at Sir Geoffry Joystick's- the list goes on. But ask any CEO, admiral, or senator and they'll confirm: rank also has its responsibilities. In the case of Skate Castle DJ, one of the tasks attendant to the role is the drop-off of daily receipts at the 3rd Street branch of Leafland Bank & Trust. And so every evening, come 8pm, Toby takes the locked pouch from Mr. Aquino and delivers it to the night drop box on his way home. Well, almost every evening.

It's not that Toby is dishonest; it's not even that he's lazy. It's just that- darn it all- sometimes Toby zigs when he should really zag. Case in point: rather than throw the trash in the alley dumpster behind his apartment yesterday morning on his way to work, Toby put it in the back of his sun-washed, canary hatchback with the intention of throwing it into the dumpster behind the Castle. Why he did this is a mystery to all but Toby, and it probably would have been fine, had he not forgotten to actually throw out the trash when he got there. Instead, distracted by a ribald exchange between callers on the radio show he was listening to while pulling into the parking lot, Toby absentmindedly left the loosely-tied bag- and its rotting contents- in the back of the car, to slowly simmer throughout the day under the bright June sky. So when 8pm rolled around, what was on Toby's mind when he got back to his car, was not that day's night drop, but rather an emergency stop at the drugstore to grab a can of air freshener and some baby wipes.

It was with mild panic and great relief that Toby was reunited this morning with yesterday's deposit bag on the passenger seat of his car. Having completely forgotten about it last night amidst the eye-stinging stink of that morning's folly, in the light of this fresh day all seemed well once again, the near-miss confirming for Toby that he walks under a lucky star. "No worries," he calmed himself cheerfully while checking his watch, "I'll just drop it off on the way in- easy peasy, problem solved." Though he'd have to hustle, so as not to be late for work...

One of the curiosities of the 3rd Street branch of Leafland Bank & Trust is that the parking lot sits atop a gentle rise in an area of otherwise flat surrounding. A fact that escaped Toby's attention, as he hopped from his car and jog-walked the locked pouch over to the drop box, hoping to right last night's wrong and get to work by 8am without anyone being the wiser; forgetting in his haste to set the parking brake. As he returned to his car Toby found it- not where he left it- but rather gaining ground and momentum as it rolled backwards through the parking lot, over a curb, across honking 3rd Street traffic, over another curb, across the neighboring parking lot, and crunching to rest against the driver's side door of some poor innocent who was inside Joe & Go grabbing their morning coffee. As he watched the show- helpless and horrified- Toby Drebber could think of nothing to do and only one thing to say: "Oops."

****

There are so many ways to break the camel's back. A flippant dismissal made by your lazy boss, one last snark from your teenage son, a salacious text misaddressed to you by your husband- these are common and well-worn straws. Sometimes it's as simple as a bad doctor's visit; other times it's more nuanced- an eyebrow raised by the wrong person at just the wrong instant, for instance. And while it's always advisable to avoid the blast zone of someone in the process of cracking, the most dangerous time is not actually at the moment of breakage, but in the moment just following: that first encounter with the just-snapped. Allow me to expound.

I entered Joe & Go this morning with much on my mind. Without going into detail, suffice it to say matters of life and death were involved- mostly death. And while in hindsight it was perhaps ill-advised to stop for coffee- and even more so to get out of the car, leaving my trunk contents unattended- in the moment I felt the need for caffeine overrode the small risk associated with a five minute detour. Unfortunately for the wide-eyed teen troglodyte manning the cash register, the combination of closed drive-thru, sleeplessness, fouled-up coffee order, wrongly-counted change, and overarching time crunch translated to that final, off-the-edge nudge. As I threw back the 37 cents that should have been 39 cents, intentionally knocked my foamless latte off the counter, and stormed out of Joe's with an admittedly-dramatic "to hell with it!" the sight that greeted me in the parking lot did my just-snapped mood no favors.

It appeared that someone had backed their rust-riddled hooptie over the curb and into the driver's side of my recently-leased, late model sedan. It wasn't a high-velocity impact, but it did its work. The driver's side door was caved in just enough to make it clear that I'd soon be visiting the body shop. And standing next to the mess- waiting, no doubt, to fan the flames of my smoldering rage- was a slack jawed schmo wearing shortsleeves, a clip-on tie, and an "aw shucks" grin. Everything about him screamed, "punch me."

By way of introduction he told me his name was DJ Drebber, he didn't know what had happened (he'd DEFINITELY set the parking brake), that he was going to push his car around mine and into the lot because it wouldn't start, and that he'd be right back. As he set to the task of shoving and grunting his sled off and around mine, he inquired over his shoulder as to the status of my insurance- the state of his own policy being somewhat dubious. He further mentioned that he was going to be late for work and would it be too much trouble for me to drop him off on my way? On my way to where he neither knew nor seemed to care. All this without a single word from me.

When I think back on the most consequential decisions of my life- those points in time where I was faced with a choice that would forever change the course of what came after- I realize, for most them I was blithely unaware at the point of choosing just how significant that moment inherently was; only in hindsight does one taste this flavor of wisdom. So was it now with DJ, as he requested a ride from a pretty little woman who likely seemed to him timid and frail, but was in truth neither.

It required laughably little of me to turn his mind away from work and toward the promise of some fantasy-fulfilled as we pulled out of the lot back to my original route, and away from whatever neon-splashed fry joint he called a job. It was equally easy to shut down his clumsy attempts at witty small talk with a few pouty lips and sultry looks. We drove in silence, but I eventually turned on the radio to cover the sounds of his mouth breathing anticipation. Desperation rose off him like fog from a moor. I don't know why I brought him with me- common sense dictates I should have left him next to the Joe & Go scratching his head with that dumb look on his face, wondering how he was going to get to work. But instead, something in me decided to make sure his day turned out to be... unusual. Plus, it's helpful sometimes to have a set of fingerprints floating around that aren't your own. So here he sits next to me now- all fidgety and unaware- rolling toward his uncertain fate. Again, beware the just-cracked.

I envy the movie knaves who always seem to have an abandoned barn or warehouse on hand in which to perform their ne'er-do-welling. What a luxury to be able to disregard the potential of prying eyes and ears; to operate without care in the light of day. The closest thing I have to private workspace is the soundproofed basement of this recently (ahem) de-occupied tract home in the suburban enclave of McDonald Ranch, roughly 20 miles from city center. It's a stick and stucco wasteland, but it's not too far out of town, the neighbors keep to themselves, and there's an enclosed garage, which lends some privacy to my comings and goings. I pull into that garage now, closing the automatic door behind me, and turning to DJ as it shuts us into darkness.

"I can't believe I'm doing this!" I say all giggly and self-conscious. "But something just wouldn't let me let you go this morning, DJ. I'm glad you're here." The dome light of the car goes on as I open my door, and in DJ's face is reflected all the hope, rejection, desire, promise, and pain of ten-plus years of cold showers and lonely nights. He's so overcome with appetite that all he can do is sit there looking at me, sparkly-eyed and gape-mouthed. "Let's go inside," I coo. "Uh-huh," he grunt-moans back to me. "I'm going to change for you- but first- be a dear and grab the bag out of the trunk for me. No peeking, Handsome, it's a surprise!" I pop the trunk and DJ dazedly walks around to the back of the car, retrieving from it the tan and orange striped vinyl bowling bag and its non-bowling related contents. He closes the trunk and crosses the garage toward me, as I flash him a "come hither" look and enter the house, through the utility room and into the kitchen.

I let him turn on the lights, grab drinks from the fridge, get glasses from the cupboard- basically encouraging him to touch as much as possible, all the while keeping sharp inventory of the few things that I'm forced to handle, and will later return to wipe down. He sips water and twitches anxiously in his seat at the kitchen table. I come up behind him, pressing my breasts gently against his back, and kiss him lightly on the cheek, whispering into his ear, "Don't worry, I'm nervous, too. Are you ready for a surprise?" He nods soundlessly. "Then open that bag and let's have some fun..."

Truth be told, I'm secretly glad that DJ ran his car into mine this morning. Dented door aside, it gave me the chance to make a new friend and bring him along for the day's adventure. Our meeting also proved a well-timed outlet to vent my Joe & Go frustration- it's almost like some mighty hand steers my course. I admit there's a part of me that wishes it didn't have to go this way for him. A part of me that wishes for his sake, he'd run when he had the chance. It's always this way, though- that flash of momentary lament- it's a voice that quiets quickly.

DJ reaches now for the zipper, and I feel my heartbeat quicken. This is it, my favorite part: The Reveal. He holds the bag with his left hand,

and slides the zipper over with his right. Engrossed in his project, DJ pulls the now-unzipped sides apart and peers curiously into the bag at its cellophane-wrapped contents. His moment of confusion is replaced in an instant with full understanding of his situation and its universe of implications. As the light of dawning realization strikes him, I slide the zip tie from my left pocket, the syringe from my right, and move in from behind: flashing toward him with a strike of my own.

****

cowboy's confession

She's my lover; I admit it. She's my illicit lover and I steal away to her every single chance I get. I love you, Arizona. I love you with a part of me so fundamental to myself that it will never go away.

And yet, I love her too. I love her like an infinite campfire ember, that glows low and orange and hot. And it never burns out. Not ever.

And I love them both with all my heart so big that it contains them both. Because this is something that happens sometimes.

Still please- don't tell Montana. I love her too much to hurt her, and I don't think she'd understand.

****

horse of a certain persuasion

A few things to know about horses... First, they can tell if a rider is comfortable in the saddle. If you're not, a horse of a certain persuasion will take advantage of the fact. It'll ignore your commands, regarding them more as the ill-conceived suggestions of a hapless nitwit who happens to be temporarily strapped to their back and is laboring under the delusion of authority, rather than the adroit directives of a skilled and confidence-inspiring equestrian, who sits tall and strong astride: a partner in adventure, an equal in enterprise. Also, some horses hate water and won't go near it, no matter what. So if you come to a river you need to cross on the back of an aquaphobic horse, it looks like some cowboy is getting wet. Another thing: you can't tug too much on a horse's reins, or it will become hard-mouthed and stop responding to commands. It's a tough condition to break, usually requiring special tack called a "hackamore" or "bitless bridle." Horses can also become hard-mouthed due to lesions or abrasions in the mouth, requiring the attention of a veterinarian. Horses have unique personalities- a truth most-evidently displayed when in a gathering, like a trail ride or on a round up. It's here you see personified a horse's desire to find and keep its spot in line. Like people, the world of horses divides into leaders and followers- and they like it that way. Try putting a horse who wants to follow in front of the line and watch you don't get kicked in the head. Put a horse who wants to lead in the rear and mind your flank doesn't have a bite taken out of it. Horses know their place.

But don't hang "horse expert" around my neck; I only know these things because I rabbit trail on the internet when I'm bored. I drilled on the topic of horses because I was heading to Arizona last spring and figured Millie would want to ride one when we got there. The only horse experience I had prior to our mildly-terrifying Tucson pony train- courtesy of the friendly-but-overpriced ranch hands at Amigo

Stables- consisted of driving past the black painted buggies of the Millersburg Amish on the way from Youngstown to Columbus to see my grandparents as a kid. I remember the ambling carriage horses wore little black blinders the size of playing cards along the sides of their faces. I asked my mom what they were for and she told me they were to shield the animals' fields of vision from the anarchy of progress. She made air quotes with her fingers at the word, "progress." Thinking back on it, her mouth was a hard line when she said it; I don't think she was being playful.

I've also drilled on the Amish. Did you know in some Amish communities, between the ages of 14 and 21, Amish kids are allowed- expected, even- to rebel against their elders? It's the time before they become full-fledged Adult Amish, when they mingle with the English and see what life is like off-res. It's true. It's called *Rumspringa.* That's German for "jumping around." Most of them stay pretty calm and lots of them don't even do it. But some of them raise holy hell: sex, drugs, rock and roll. Some of them go bananas. They can come back to the farm anytime they like before the window closes- no questions asked. If they do something super messed up- like kill a guy- the community has to take them back and hide them. But if they try to come back after time runs out, well... no dice. Total excommunicado. Sometimes the final departed change their minds and are so desperate to come home they have to be run off by their family with a pitchfork. It can get harsh. Again, this is all information available to anyone with a computer and a connection, so don't give me too much credit; I'm just passing along information here. The only parts you might have a little trouble verifying are the stuff about killing the guy and the pitchfork stuff. I didn't make it up, *per se*, I just extrapolated a bit. And I don't think it's a stretch- more an acknowledgement of the natural consequences of these ideas. Think about it, if you lock a person up for most of their life, then send them off into the wild without supervision or context, what do you think is going to happen? And if they do go out and mess up real bad, isn't it on you to help them out? Like I said, natural consequences.

It's kind of a hobby of mine to think about outcomes for things people do. I like to watch them, then see what happens and compare it to what I thought was going to happen. You know, like, "There goes A doing B. I thought C was going to happen; didn't see D coming..." I find people a constant source of amusement- they're always surprising you with bad choices. Millie thinks it's poor form to analyze people without them knowing, but I tell her it's the purest form of social science. How else do you avoid making the same mistake twice? Here's an example:

There was this girl in high school named Quinley, but everyone called her Candy because she was so sweet. And also because her dad drove a windowless van that looked like something a kidnapper would hand candy out of. He was a painter- houses and walls, not canvases. So anyhow, Candy was really into politics. She loved government and history and all that jazz. She was whip-smart, too. Ended up getting a scholarship, and went back East for college. She comes home one summer to do an internship at Senator Best's office- the younger one, not the older one- and she becomes friends with one of the staffers, a girl named Charlie. Charlie shows her the ropes- takes her to meetings, introduces her to donors, teaches her the lingo- that kind of stuff. These two are getting along great and everyone on the staff really likes Candy- she might even get a full-time job offer when she graduates. So one day Charlie takes Candy to the monthly Weapons & Self-defense Freedom rally down at Iron Fist Lake. If you've never been it's a laid back deal; no one's there to make trouble, just tailgate and gel, and maybe squeeze a few off into the air during the group Trigger Pull. So everything is cool and people are just hanging out, and then a group of eugenics advocates show up and start handing out fliers and chatting up the crowd. Candy winds up in conversation with a guy espousing the genetic superiority of the Indo-Canadians and she can't help but think he might be onto something. Her opinion colored in some part- no doubt- by the results of the DNA field test he swabs her with right there next to the lake. In 40 minutes of talking, this guy changes her whole world view. So what does Candy do? The next morning she heads into the Senator's office and quits on the spot. Then she flies back to DC, changes her major to Genomic Assemblage with a minor in Canadian Lineage, and three months later she's dead. Looked the wrong way stepping off a curb and got creamed by an electro-tram. And there you have it: natural consequences.

Millie hates that story- says it does nothing to prove my point, and if anything, only highlights the ephemeral and capricious nature of life. I tell her she's thinking too small. In order to really get the point, you have to see life in the Meta, as a web of interconnected events. Each idea and action setting to motion its own unique set of ramifications- as mysterious as intuition, as unavoidable as death. To this Millie retorts I'm describing Karma, not culmination; it's a claim I don't dispute.

Another of my hobbies is droning. You know, remote-controlled flying cameras. On some level I guess, it's the natural progression from liking to watch people make decisions at ground level. With a drone, you get to watch them make decisions from the air. If you get high enough, sometimes you can even see patterns forming- kinda like social fractals. When I first got into it about eight years ago, I started off at the park, flying self-made obstacle courses and recording dogs playing fetch, kids running, couples picnicking- parky things. That got boring pretty quick, though, and I started to seek new avenues. I dabbled in racing clubs, high altitude nature photography, I even made a little money doing restricted fly-overs for real estate video listings. But none of these applications let me do what I really wanted to with my drone, which was watch people from above. The main problem was that people largely live in cities, and cities generally don't allow drones. This unfortunate truth pushed me into one of the pastime's shaded corners: guerilla droning.

Really, "guerilla droning" is just a menacing-sounding term invented by hobbyists who are trying to make their weekends sound daring. All it means is flying one's toy where it's not supposed to be. In the early days of the recreation, pro-droners had the edge over the anti-droners. No one really knew what drones were capable of, and rules didn't yet exist to control the behavior. Repercussions were of the "stop or I'll say 'stop' again" variety. But in time, the system began to favor the Antis. Not only were laws changed to prohibit the use of drones in urban areas, but counter-drone technology improved, too. Now, in addition to running afoul of the law, if you droned in the wrong neighborhood, you might find your very expensive toy brought down and destroyed by an enterprising vigilante with a parabolic disrupter or a bola rifle. Anti-droning actually became its own form of amusement. It added some spice to the sport, but a lot of cost, too. Nearly all skychimps (slang for guerilla dronists), eventually run out of money and/or patience for replacing downed drones. In my case, it was after my fifth machine was taken out- this time by a net gun- that I decided it was time to leave the city and head for the hills.

Transitioning from urban to provincial surveillance requires some patience, but it's well-worth the effort. People are everywhere in the city, so you don't have to work very hard to find something to watch. There's a lot more hunting and pecking in the open space of the country, but the rewards are greater because the finds are so much wackier. Many people go to the country to be not-seen, so when you do happen upon them, they're generally more unfiltered in their behavior, because they think they're alone. Again, Millie disapproves, but I just can't help to be fascinated by what people get themselves up to. I've found drug farms, nudist enclaves, and crop mazes, as well as all variety of backwoods ceremony: nuptial, sacrificial, initiation, maturation, inhumation, matriculation, and expulsion- to name a few. I've seen things buried, smoked, drunk, set to fire, and dismembered. I've seen banquets, brawls, and orgies. To tell you true, I thought I'd seen it all- I thought nothing could surprise me; but what I stumbled onto recently proved me very, very wrong.

About six weeks ago I was grid-scanning a remote quadrant of Parcel 41, northwest of Fernie, when I happened over a pasture that caught my eye. The field was obviously man made- a fact made evident by its approximate 25 square acre shape, cut sharply from the middle of an otherwise vast expanse of impenetrable forest. Also eye-catching was the game trail that criss-crossed through the green-groomed and perfectly square meadow in a perfectly X'ed pattern. Based on its distinct outlines, it was clear to me that the path was well-used, though there were no animals to be seen. The meadow's boundary was unfenced and no roads led to or from it; a paddock singularly unique for its meticulous design and inaccessible installation. I was captivated. I started flying over it daily, then twice daily, then nearly constantly- pausing my observations only long enough to recharge the drone and perform maintenance on the engine and rotors. Day flying led to night flying, as I swapped the full-light optics for low light/no light lenses, and IR and heat signature packages. Eventually, I just set the drone to "constant hover" and used a motion sensing lens. I was obsessed with discovering who was responsible for this impossible sward, its straight razor lines, and the well-worn paths that crossed it. But despite all my time, effort and creativity, I saw nothing... until I saw something.

For those unacquainted with the lunar cycle, every month of the year has one full moon, making twelve per year. Every two or three years there's an additional full moon, a thirteenth known as the "Blue Moon." Similar to the periodic "Blue," every month's full moon has a nickname. For example, in January, it's a "Wolf Moon," in May, a "Hare Moon," in August, a "Corn Moon." Et cetera. The nickname for October's full moon is "Blood Moon," and it happens to have occurred eight days ago. It also happens to mark the night that over a month's worth of field surveillance paid off. I was returning to station after a couple hours' worth of rejuicing the batteries and a lovely-but-all-too-brief sandwich and root beer with Millie. The combination of night optics and the Blood Moon's full light had the field glowing like a stadium on my live-feed monitor. Despite the perfect visibility, I was so used to seeing an empty screen that it took me a minute to understand something was happening. I literally rubbed my eyes when I saw it. Filing in steady stream from the north and south corners of the meadow's east side- perfectly spaced and in perfect cadence- were two lines of cows. They were pouring onto the pasture from some unseen wellspring in the woods, one after the other. The northeast line of cows was moving diagonally across the field toward its southwest corner, and the southeast line was heading to the northwest corner. They moved in unison, nose to tail, and were uniformly spaced one cow length apart, each from the next. When the two lines crossed at the field's interpunct, the lines passed and moved perfectly through each other. Never a disruption to the movement. Nary a stumble, nary a bump. Everything about their movements was identical- even their legs moved in perfect concert. Ever seen 50,000 Chinese soldiers marching in a parade? It was just like that: flawless, hypnotic, slightly comical. Terrifying. I yelled for Millie to come see, but she'd already headed out, so I sat there by myself watching in increasing and captivated horror as cow after cow marched out of the wood and across the field with machine-like orchestration.

After about 30 minutes of marching, the cavalcade was complete, the forest emptied, and every cow was to its place. Then- arguably- what happened next turned things even stranger, because nothing happened. The herd just stood there- motionless- each cow staring straight ahead at the cow before it, without so much as a chew of cud, or a swish of tail. Total stillness. Like a collection of statues marked out in a perfect 'X' across the middle of a perfect field, in the middle of exactly nowhere.

Following 45 minutes of watching cows watch other cows do nothing, I started to get a little twitchy and decided to drop down for a closer look. This was a mistake. I'd been hovering at 500 feet in "whisper mode" and had to switch off the baffles to maneuver in. Now cows don't have the hearing of- say- a bat, but they hear better than humans do, and when the drone started emitting its telltale buzz of descent, my heretofore invisible vantage was compromised. Best guess puts about 400 cows in that field, and at the first sound of my drone, the head of every single one of them snapped up in perfect unison and looked directly through my hi-res camera, straight into my eyes. Perfect unison. Every single one. Before my mind could even register what was happening, the screen flashed white, then went dead black. The connection was cut; all contact with the drone was lost, and the flight controller in my hands was rendered worthless as stone. I must have sat there for another 10 minutes or so- dumb and numb- shocked stupid by the creepy weirdness of it all. Then I reached for the 'rewind' toggle to prove to myself what I'd just seen. But here's another thing: none of it saved. Despite the fact that I watched the whole thing stream through on my live feed, when I went back to rewatch the footage, there was nothing there, not even static. So far as concerns posterity, none of it ever happened.

It would be gross understatement to say all of this unnerved me. I called Millie in a bit of a panic and she hustled back over- I think she could hear the fraying sanity in my voice. My biggest source of terror wasn't the zombie cow parade, the freaky look of other-than-nothing they gave me when they gazed up into my camera, or even the missing recording. What bothered me most about it all was the impossibility of what I'd seen. I don't like things that can't be explained. Like so many, I rely on logic to make sense of my world. Without explanation, all of this experience is a swirling abyss of random occurrence. That will not do.

When Millie arrived I brought her back to my control room and told her the whole story. Then I showed her the dead flight controller and nonexistent vid files. She sat for a moment in thoughtful silence, then gave me the best advice I never took: let it go. There are forces at work here that are best left be; ignore the temptation that not knowing presents, and let it go. But my damnable ego deafened me to this sagacity.

I spent the next three days in maniacal study, researching everything I could get my hands on that came anywhere near the geo coordinates of that field. All manner of government record, petition, fiat, warrant, grant, and deed. I studied topographical charts, geological records, logging and forest service maps, and every satellite image I could get my hands on. It may not surprise you to hear- as I was on some level unsurprised to discover- nothing about this field could be found: no record, no mention, no photo- nothing. The location in question was but a drop in a sea of undeveloped, untamed, and largely inaccessible government land. Millie sat by through all of this, watching with increasing concern as I worked with increasing agitation in the waxing light of a dawning realization: as like the video footage, the field does not exist.

It's not Millie's way to threaten or beg, but she came pretty close to both when trying to dissuade me from the course I endeavored upon in the wake of my research. It was then I set out to see for myself this place of non-being. Armed with a geocompass and four days of backcountry provisions, by means of abandoned service roads I penetrated as deeply as I could into the barbarous woods- toward the coordinates of my white whale- before running out of road and trading truck for foot. From there I picked up any game trail that moved me even roughly toward my destination- a circuitous pre-worn path being in all ways preferable to the savagery of a direct line in this impossibly dense wood. When game trails gave out, the true slog began, as I scraped and clawed my way over and through forest so close-packed and unforgiving that at times I had to take off my pack and squeeze between trees to make forward progress. I set to foot five days ago, I saw the last of trails three days ago. I arrived at the field's coordinates five minutes ago. I started to lose hope four minutes ago.

There's nothing here. Correction: there's nothing here but forest and felled forest and rocks and more forest. There is no field, there are no trails, there are no cows. There is no treasure of great revelation. From where I stand, there is barely sky. I had such high hopes for this adventure, but none of what I promised myself has obtained. I imagined my victorious return from the wild, rich with knowledge that would reshape the path of all peoples. I imagined Millie's proud look and my gentle joshing: "See," I'd tease, "I told you it would be alright." But instead, here I am: a fool in the wild, ignoring good advice, chasing vain ambition, and running out of options. I don't know what I saw on that screen, and I don't know why it's all gone now. But I do know this: despite what you tell yourself, despite what you hope- some stories don't end the way you want them to.

I wish I'd never looked. I want to go home.

****

fast-arrived the crash

For all the love we showed it, all the materiality we gave it, all the time and energy we invested in talking about it, thinking about it, it's amazing how fast-arrived the crash of Sport. One day we were all geared up: tip to tail in our colors, screaming like maniacs for our guys, high-fiving and beer guzzling from the stands while sharing that electrified air of contest. Then, in the blink of an eye we were watching the dramatics from afar, cheering half-heartedly from the anticlimactic isolation of our sofas as feats of strength and speed were performed by masked strangers in empty arenas, before cardboard cut-outs, to the sounds of canned applause.

We held out hope that we could bring it back "after this craziness settles," but the further away we got from how it had been, the harder it proved to steer that ship back to shore. The whole thing was much more delicately balanced than anyone realized. Part of it was that all the carefully crafted drama needed an audience to fuel it. Heroes and villains play best before a live studio audience. But also, the entire enterprise was extremely resource intensive. Massive amounts of money, huge facilities, giant chunks of airtime and bandwidth undergirded the machine. As time went on, means dwindled across the board and priorities started to rejig. And thus Goliath was felled by a sneeze.

What never did go away was our collective need for triumph and subjugation: the thrill of victory, the agony of defeat, et cetera and so forth. So we needed a proxy for all that lost pageantry, something to fill the hole left by our human need to compete, to win, and- sometimes- to lose. A few candidates threw their hat in the ring. First came video gaming: a high-def replication of that which was lost. The visuals were immaculate, the representation of the icons and their movements flawless. But even the best technology couldn't hide that the new behind-the-scenes heroes of the game were at heart- and often in actuality- basement dwellers, quick-thumbed-though-otherwise-unremarkable Normals; and there just wasn't enough there to worship. Gambling was the next logical substitute, and for a while it thrived- but soon faltered, too. Beyond the endurance required to sit at a table for hours on end, there was no real physicality involved, and turns out an element of athleticism was needed to hold everyone's attention. If a chain smoking 80-year-old could dominate from a motorized wheelchair, that just wasn't sporting enough for the masses. As time drew on and things became increasingly desperate, even mano a mano bloodsport enjoyed a temporary renaissance. Dueling swords scratched a few itches. There was the convenient forum offered for the airing of grievances. (So long as duels were authorized by the appropriate governing bodies, all was considered fair play.) And certainly skill and physical acumen played major roles. Problem was, there was no star power. Either the best ran out of beef to squash, or they ran out of luck. Whatever the case, there were just too many new faces getting run through for rule-bound violence to stay a thing. Though it took a while, eventually this vacuum was filled; it came from a familiar but unexpected quarter. Behold: the Rise of Carnival.

Amazing we didn't gravitate to it sooner, but maybe that's just hindsight talking. Carnival has all the qualities of the surrogate we needed: heroes, villains, chance, skill, and thrill. Even the food is good. There were a few wrinkles to be ironed out. For one, there wasn't enough sex appeal. Carnies don't generally fan the flame of desire for most people, and we'd come to expect an element of the libidinous in our sport. And the venues were too constricting for a populace that was skittish and reeling from years of contagion, paranoia, and quarantine. Plus, Carnival- while fun to play and laugh along with- was really not a spectator event, in the familiar sense. But these all proved to be solvable problems.

As for venue, in the wake of Sport's demise, the world was sitting on pitch after field after stadium of empty place; massive edifices and wide open spaces begging for the return of competitive energy. Plenty of room to set up, plenty of room to spread out. Regarding sex, it also proved a relatively easy fix. As Carnival gained its grip, so did its audience swell and its reputation as a legitimate concern grow.

This widened the bosses' window to attract the more attractive. In other words, as Carnival became more popular, carnies became better looking. The spectator nut was a little tougher to crack, but as games and prizes evolved, the crowds waxed and the people watched. Game Show fanfare proved a helpful model, as cupie dolls and goldfish were in time replaced by much shinier gauds.

It took more than a nice stadium, good looks, and a new car to rise to the top of the watchlist, however. Carnival had always been competitive- the best barkers ever brought the biggest crowds. But add money to the mix- real money, big money- and Carnival became downright cutthroat. As in all high stakes games, some little fish became big fish and some big fish became dinner. After a period of skirmish and gain, the carnival world was winnowed to an oligarchy of five global titans.

Western Europe was claimed by the Irish-Romani vagabond Laszlo O'Keefe: a man of flexible virtue and iron will, who affirmed himself the unconfirmed offspring of a knife-thrower and a unicyclist; born in the alley of a Rue Saint Denis absinthe house, "sometime before the war." Begun as a small-time promoter, O'Keefe built his empire one tent at a time, acquiring exhibition after exhibition, until his company boasted over 35,000 performers and game captains dotted across Europe and North Africa. Word on the street is, he buried more than a few bodies along the way. A self-described "pikey made good," no number of Savile Row suits or Swiss-made watches will ever hide the snake eyes or fast-flowing lilt of this true blue grinder.

To the right of Laszlo lies the empire of Eastern European carnivalcrat Zoya Kruchina. Twenty-five years ago, Zoya inherited a modest circus outfit from her father, Yuri, which she then endeavored to build into the most ruthless cadre of gaffers, dukkers, fixers, flatties, didicoys, hawkers, boss hostlers, butchers, menders, and joggerin' omis in the Northern Hemisphere. Drawing from the western world's richest traditions of contortion and sleight-of-hand, Ms. Kruchina's talent pool is legendary, as is her expectation of loyalty. Few of her corps ever leave her for other carnivals, and those that do are not only black-balled by her 40,000 strong "Zoyistas", but hunted as fugitives across the globe. Though it's rare for a Zoyista to defect, it's common for those that dare to wake up in a foreign camp with a slit throat. As they say in the cult of Carnival Kruchina, "Zoya play for keep."

If the western world of carnival is evenly cleaved between Laszlo and Zoya, the eastern half of this orb is much more blurred and bloodied; for the lines of demarcation here are not nearly as clean or respectfully observed between its rivaled leviathans.

In the western East rose the next of the world's five midway masters; his name is Sai Singh. Born eighth of eleven siblings near a trash heap in Kolkata, his departed parents' only bequest unto him was wit, an estate he put to purposeful employment. Sai dug himself from the filth of his inception with a deck of cards, grifting rupees enough as an abstemious street hustler to seed a small rickshaw outfit, employing his siblings as drivers. This small rickshaw outfit in time grew to become a massive rickshaw outfit, which Sai- in his prescience- parlayed into the ascendant world of Carnival, selling the rickshaws to buy a controlling stake in a near-bankrupt games and rides maker in Mumbai. As equipment supplier to Asia's countless festivals, fairs, and bazaars, Sai built his empire from the inside out- starting in India then spreading east to China and beyond. Always with an eye for a deal, Sai was able to acquire a collection of struggling customers and assemble them into a 25,000-tent strong juggernaut of amusement that he sibilantly self-styled, 'Sai Singh's Circus.' A lion among kittens, Sai's rocketship is fueled by grit, cold blood, and twelve hours of sleep a week. He is an apex predator without threat or rival. But for one.

While Sai was clawing his way through the Kolkata muck, silk-clad Ma Jin was sipping broth from his amah's jade spoon in a Macau penthouse. The only child of gaming magnate and Beijing darling, Ma Bing, Jin was raised at the knee of Asia's gambling elite and quickly developed a reputation as a math genius and pai gow wunderkind. Following the Hong Kong purge and entrenchment, Jin- then a piss and vinegar-soaked twenty-something- was sent by his father to oversee the construction of a gaming and entertainment district in Kowloon: a Party-sanctioned propitiation (and social distraction) for the peninsula's recently-quelled. It was during this period that Jin was introduced to the world of carnival, its untapped potential, and the rising reign of Sai Singh. Seeing the opportunity- and loving a good fight- Jin secured the support of his father, handed off Hong Kong, then went to work building his army of hustlers and geeks. From there, the story gyres to one of operatic intrigue, murder, and clash between the warring dynasties of Singh and Ma for control of Asia's carnival crown.

But for all the wealth and power these lords wield over their respective realms, only one truly sits atop the stack. She needs but a single name to be known. That name is Calliope, and her show of traveling wonders is Ravenwood.

Say you head due south from Yellowknife, down through the Dakotas, across the Great Plains and down; down through Omaha, Topeka, Austin- over the Rio Grande- and along the bugle of Mexico: Monterrey, Guanajuato, Villahermosa, and beyond. Say you keep going down; down through Tegucigalpa, Managua, San Jose. Keep going. Down, more down. Medellín, Quito; then wet your boots in the Amazon and keep going down. Rio Branco, La Paz, and Santa Cruz. Now rest your head in Asunción, but don't loiter long, for you still have 4,000 klicks to go before you run out of road and travel the full meridian of Calliope's rule.

Her domain is massive, her wealth beyond count, and her sway untold. But for all the scope and gold, Calliope's greatest source of renown is- ironically- her mystery. A New Orleans accent belies her São Paulo aspect, but that's as close as anyone has come to pinning her origin. A private jet is her home and she flies it, with loose itinerary, from pole to pole and coast to coast across her Americas, dropping in on Ravenwood's myriad midways to "see how things are going" and occasionally be the star of the show.

For though her menagerie of enchantment spans a staggering swath- in a pleasant afternoon of Ravenwood wandering one can place a wager on a racing giraffe, watch the blue whale do tricks, ooh and aah at a one-armed juggler tossing (and hardly ever dropping) newborns, cheer along at a dog fight, then snack on balut and snake wine- it's rumor of a Calliope appearance that really swells the crowds beyond capacity.

Amazement is the only expectation when Calliope performs, as every time the delights are different, and her skills- to hear it told- are myriad. Witnesses attest: she can eat glass, move through walls, land on her feet from a 10-story fall, fight bears to the death, see your past, know your future, light fire with a look, freeze water with a word, and kill with a thought. Rumor has it, Calliope is not of this world; and by all appearances, rumor is right.

But it's not the hope of glimpsing Calliope's theurgy that brings me this day down Ravenwood's hall of merriment. Nor the promise of seeing some exotic creature performing acts, nor the sight of a freak exposing God's twisted humor, nor even the chance to wrench my guts in freefall on some impossible ride. I steer the squeals and screams of this reimagined golf course-now-carnival, this fairway midway, if you will, on a more pedestrian errand: I seek to win a game of chance.

Ravenwood offers many ways to try your hand at snatching the pocketbook of Lady Luck. Old standards abound: cards, coins, cups & balls. But it's the more modern twists that I prefer. Some time back it was determined that while dime pitch and duck pond serve well a certain set, there is a portion of the carnival crowd that seeks a higher-stakes buzz, and for these thrill-seekers, new games were needed.

They crept slow from the shadows; it wasn't initially known how much tolerance the crowd would have for contests involving true risk. The purses escalated quickly, but that only entertained the horde for so long- what's a million lost to one who can afford to lose it? And anyhow, high rollers had been losing big money since time immemorial- nothing new there. Things didn't really take off until blood was drawn. After all, the kink for the big stakes crowd has always had more to do with avoiding the loss than relishing the win.

Blood but trickled at first. It started with healable wounds (broken noses and jaws), then elevated to scars and limps (knife to cheek, bat to knee), before moving onto low-level deformities (expendable digits, i.e. pinkies and toes). Of course with each escalation of damage, the rewards escalated in lockstep. By the time thumbs were being bartered, the payoffs were matching half a decade's worth of working man's salary- a risk worth taking for many. A risk worth watching for nearly all. But still, there was yet lower for the mind to descend, and yet higher for the stakes to climb.

Of course anyone watching knew where this was headed: you can't pay more than your life. What was uncertain wasn't so much the destination, as the path to get there. It was the war between Singh and Ma- their arms race of one upmanship- that engendered the concept of commercializing Russian roulette and putting it in front of a crowd. It was Calliope's ingenuity that had her refashioning the game into "The Devil's Progressive" and turning it into the hottest ticket on Earth.

Here's the bag...

Traditional Russian roulette- Singh and Ma's Russian roulette- involves one live round, a six-chambered handgun, a spun cylinder, a quick olive branch offered to whatever god you've forsaken, and a trigger squeezed. For the opportunity to play, punters pay that day's market price for five ounces of gold. For the opportunity to watch, spectators pay the equivalent of one. If the gun goes 'click' instead of 'bang,' the lucky fool makes 1000 times his money. If not, well... someone grab a mop. Carnies have their fun.

The Devil's Progressive flips the script. Rather than buying one round and five empty chambers, here you buy one empty chamber and five rounds. Price to play with Calliope: twenty-five ounces of gold. Price to watch: ten. For those tracking the math, the odds swap from an 83% chance of 'click' in Russian roulette to an 83% chance of 'bang' at Ravenwood. But every bloody cloud has a silver lining. Where Singh-Ma success pays a paltry 1000 times money, Ravenwood pays the pot. Which is to say, everytime Calliope's cleanup crew rolls out, the payout rolls up. The pot includes all previously-failed players' entry fees, plus ten percent of the in-house take. Calliope keeps all pay-per-view and merchandising revenues. She's not running a charity, after all. At last count, the Ravenwood progressive for 'suicide roulette' (the showman's sobriquet for the game) was nearing 400 million United States dollars.

But still, you ask, what madness drives one to take such unmitigated risk? Surely no promise of any amount of money is worth the near-certainty of failure, of death? You'd be surprised. Consider this hypothetical:

Imagine you're 48 years old. Imagine you have three kids- precious angels each- 8, 10 and 10. Two girls and a boy. Imagine you're married to a woman who always knows how to make you laugh, always shows you the adventure in life. Your shotgun rider, your best friend. So far, so good? Good. Now imagine a year ago you were caught in the gears of a downsize, and- but for the ante you've somehow managed to scrape together (by virtue of selling all you own and taking out loans you can't repay)- you're flat broke. Imagine you've just discovered that inside your skull burrows and squirms an incurable malignancy so insidious that the prospect of a bullet smashed through your brain in front of

5,000 screaming strangers, on live television watched by millions more, is a scenario preferable to that which lies ahead for you, your wife, your two girls and a boy. Imagine what it would feel like to leave your wife widowed, your children fatherless, your family penniless. Imagine your options and what you'd choose. Hypothetically speaking.

The stage is remarkably nondescript, considering the tapestry of drama that's soon to hereupon unfurl. It's really no more than a raised platform, canvas-covered and sawdust-strewn. Think: little boxing ring, without the ropes. On the stage is a single side table, no chair. This is not a sitting game. Upon the table sit a revolver and a box of 50 shells, though just five are needed (and really, only one). Raised seating surrounds the dais, giving 360 degrees of audience a direct view. Live-stream cameras afix from every angle. The lighting is perfect.

I vaguely remember walking to the stage and up its three short steps by way of a narrow aisle that parted a hushed and electrified crowd and had as its trailhead a dingy backstage locker room. It's there I received instructions, the only one that registered being, "Aim up. You don't want to take anyone with you, you know..."

You wouldn't let a carnie pack your chute, and for similar reasons, in this game you load your own gun. The bullets feel heavy in my hand, portentous. My hands are mercifully steady and the rounds slide in easily, almost eagerly, like they want to get this over with, too. There's a barker spieling something, but I'm not listening. Whatever she's saying, it has the effect of unstupefying the crowd and frothing them to frenzy. It's almost time to go. She leads them in a rousing countdown: "10!...9!...8!...7!...6!"

...I could tell you I'm seized by the terror of having my existence hang by the most slender filament. I could tell you my thoughts have distilled down to the most fundamental memories of love: my child's laugh, my wife's touch...

"5!...4!"

...but that would be a lie. In truth, my thoughts are nothing, my mind blank. I just want to know, what's it going to be: click, or bang? Let's find out...

"3!...2!!...1!!!"

Game time.

****

say something about love

"Say something about love," she said.

Ok, imagine this... A tool with slicing edge and good grip. A stabbing, ripping thing suitable for defense and offense. Add heat: steel red bending rock melting sweat dripping hair wet sheet soaking slick sliding heat. Find what's kicking off that heat and put your face up against it. Don't pull away until the skin boils and you smell hair. Now take your fire-wrecked face and dunk it in cool, perfect water (limpid, rejuvenate, inspiriting). Keep it there for a bit. Sleep. Burrow in and slumber in fresh, shaded breeze. The water and rest heal you to scar.

All this is something like love.

****

her face blushes titian

Her face blushes titian from the dying coals' reflected glow. She sits close to the hearth- we both do- trying to absorb as much warmth as we can in the moments remaining, before the fire ebbs out, heat departs, and our only light becomes a warmless candle between us. Some respite is offered from the frigid cold by the trapper's blankets we found, in the battered wardrobe we found, in the one-room cabin we found, in the woods where we recklessly wandered, just before the angry sky swung its stormhammer down upon us.

It looks to be some city dweller's offgrid summer hermitage: poorly insulated and ill-equipped for the mountain's real weather. But it has a fireplace, a couple of blankets, and a single log to burn. The cupboards are bare- provisions most likely carted in and out by the owners for July and August sojourns- and but for a handful of left-behind stores, the place is merely a clapboard shell. Fortunately for us, among these scant "essentials" are included the two aforementioned blankets, three candles, a book of matches, and a heavily thumbed copy of an old dictionary, the pages of which provided a much-needed starter to getting that log lit. Thank goodness for the English tongue. Don't think for a second we look this gift horse in the mouth: in the whiteout that rages just beyond the pinewood door, this place is quite literally a lifesaving shelter.

Emergency situations don't usually abide awkwardness, but I have to admit that as I sit across the cold floor from this girl, amidst our progressively deteriorating circumstances, it's a little weird between us. Fact is, I really don't know her very well. Sure we've spent the last few years flitting and flirting around each other at work- flashing looks of increasingly long duration at one another, laughing a little too loudly in project meetings at the other's limp witticisms, and finding excuses to happen across each other's path any time we could do it without seeming obvious- but our connection is largely anchored to the physical, and that's not necessarily the best foundation when a state of affairs distills down to life and death. "Cold," she chatters from between the folds of her woolen cocoon. "Yup," I chatter back from between the folds of mine.

Perfect universal alignment was required to bring us to this place in time. A chance meeting in the break room on Friday afternoon led to Chrissy's offhand invitation for a Saturday hike. An ill-timed argument with my girlfriend on Friday morning led me to accept. A Saturday morning pocket dial from my sister distracted me away from checking the day's weather on my way out the door. A fluke collision of air masses gathered over the North Range led to this early season superstorm. And on and on it goes.

Not counting my dogs Thor and Strudel, and in addition to the passing of Oma, Pop Pop, and Grandpa Clem, I've had three close encounters with Death in my 32 years. The first was when I was eight. I saw a kid get hit by a truck. He ran after a ball into an intersection, and that was that. The second was my neighbor and childhood best friend, Lars. Lymphoma got him when we were 17. Worst day of my life. The third was my own near miss when I was 26 and living over in Stetson. I fell asleep driving home after a rowdy night out with the girls. Wrapped my car around a tree, somehow managing to hobble away with only a broken arm and 18 stitches across my hairline. Absolute miracle. I bring this up only because I have a sneaking suspicion that Encounter Number Four is lurking somewhere nearby, out in the screaming storm, just beyond that pinewood door.

Conversation in the cabin has stalled out. When we first broke into the place- after hours of initially playful, then mildly concerned, then tensely fearful, then out-and-out panicked forest wandering- our close call was celebrated with a slew of nervous prattle. We laughed, we hugged, we even danced around a little, thinking naively that danger was past and our path to safety but a smooth glide home. As we back-slapped and gabbed in the cold-sieved shanty, the tempest outside roiled and swelled- gathering itself up for the Big Exhale. Once the storm's full force arrived, our chatty celebration diffused itself to a tenor of somber quietude.

Now I've had better days, but Chrissy looks downright unwell. She's shivering uncontrollably- almost violently, her hands are having trouble keeping the blanket wrapped up, and she's starting to nod off intermittently. I'm no doctor, but my guess is that she's in the early stages of hypothermia. I have no idea what to do about it. Again, I'm no doctor.

My mom used to do this thing when my sister and I were kids where anytime we were really upset she'd distract us with a totally non sequitur story. For example, if we'd come home crying with a skinned knee or bruised ego, in a few moments of hearing her imaginings, all tears would be gone and any hurt forgotten as we were immersed in Mom's tale of, *"The Time Her Cousin Tommy Lopped His Pinky Finger Off With A Pizza Cutter When He Was At University,"* or, *"The Time Pop Pop Spanked Her For Breaking A Window At The Hansen's Place After Being Told Not To Throw Rocks At The Chickens."* Sometimes she'd freestyle, making up silly stories off the top of her head, trying each time to outdo herself in ridiculousness. *"Professor Pickle Britches And The Mystery Of The Cross-eyed Unicorn"* was one of my favorites. *"Fru Jacobsen And The Haunted Bratwurst"* another. My adolescent will and pride always fought hard to stay upset, but Mom- never one to be deterred- would stay at it until the story overwhelmed the indignation. It was a masterful tactic and I always appreciated the effort. In fact, this might be a good time to try it out myself- seems Chrissy and I could both use a little distraction.

"You know who Skadi is, right?" I ask Chrissy's still and huddled form. The blanketed lump sits silent, so I ask again. Still no answer. I ask a third time, more loudly now. "Chrissy? Chrissy! You know Skadi- the snow huntress- you know who I mean?" "What? Skadi? What are you talking about?" Chrissy mumbles back- like a just-roused drunk. "Skadi- you know her? The goddess of snow and ski, protectress of Scandinavia- you know who I'm talking about?" I persist. Chrissy stirs, clears slightly, then answers, "Yeah, I...I know Skadi." "Well do you know she had a sister?" I ask. "What? No, I guess I didn't know that," Chrissy replies, equal parts engaged and confused. Emboldened by her slow-building lucidity, I continue. "Well she did. Her name was Astrid, and by all reports, she and Skadi were quite the rabble-rousers."

"Oh?" goes Chrissy. (There's the bite; now to set the hook.) "Oh, indeed," I reply, then begin...

****

It was once so that there lived two enchanted princesses, named Skadi and Astrid. They were half sisters- born of different mothers, but samely sired by the powerful sky king, Freyr- and each was endowed with fabled magic and beauty. Skadi- the eldest- was a mighty goddess who ruled over Snow and Vengeance. She was much praised and feared by the mountain clans, for they lived by her whims and suffered her displeasure. Astrid- the younger- was known to command the stars, and so was greatly revered by sailors who steered the night sky's celestial light. The sisters lived with their father in a fortress of gabbro and gold high among the mountains of Nur. Because King Freyr was the temple god of Peace and Fair Weather, he was often prayed down from the high peaks into the vales and fjords below to soothe tempers among clashing septs and lend safe passage to pious travelers, leaving Skadi and Astrid to the cold, empty palace and their lonesome devices.

During one such stretch when their father was away, the sisters took to squabbling- as sisters will sometimes do- and argued over who was the mightier goddess. "As I command all ice and snow," said Skadi, "... surely I am the stronger." "Nay," answered Astrid back, "...as the will of the stars bend to me, 'tis I who am clearly the greater." No argument swayed, so it was decided between them that a contest was needed, and they devised a tournament of three trials to see which witch was weaker, and which would win.

First they tested fleetness and flash, and so the sisters raced from the castle's courtyard, down Nur's steep-peaked side, to the seashore at valley's edge- far below. Each chose a means of travel: Skadi raced by ski, and Astrid by sled. The sisters roared down the mountain's icy face, razing all in their path, and leaving in their wake a trail of flame and mist. Once settled the steam, Skadi was revealed the victor, and scoffed down her little sister, teasing lightly, "See then, Astrid- though you are fast, I am faster, and clearly the greater god." Astrid fought back her frustration at losing and spoke softly to her big sister, saying, "We shall see, Skadi, we shall see..."

Then next the sisters vied to show their command of wind and sky. Skadi- going first- bawled to the heavens a terrible howl, entreating it to throw down its power and dislodge a slab of stone that tumbled violently through the gorges of Nur, killing everything in its path.

Nodding in praise of her sister's magic, Astrid went next, raising her arms and chanting the empyrean black and swirling. She called down a barrage of thunder that raged like war and shook the very mountain itself, flooding through the valley an avalanche so wide and raving, that it left nothing behind but stumps and stone, and buried the seaside village below in 1000 hands of snow. "See then, Sister," spoke Astrid with a smile, "...who's might is most." Skadi, in admiration of her sister's strength, conceded this defeat.

And so the contest reduced to its final feat: a test of mortal domination and fear. But before the sisters could begin their determinate trial, their father-king returned from his pilgrimage- and he was in a rage. "How now, Daughters!?" he furied. "What mischief is this that finds my mountainside ravaged and my sea village destroyed?" Quaking in apprehension of his wrath, the sisters fell at their father's feet and begged his mercy, but Freyr was unmoved by their contrition. "I will show you the same charity you showed my people, Child Queens!" bellowed Freyr, the God of Peace and Sun. "It's trials you like, so it's trials you get," he spoke to his daughters- his anger settling, but his resolve entrenched...

****

I pause here, letting my storyteller's far-off gaze return to the scene before me, refocusing on my gelid surroundings, and- more specifically- Chrissy's state of being. Things have not improved. She's shivering less- a datum I take at first for good, though I quickly realize this is due only to a decline of her condition. Her hands no longer clasp the blanket- it drapes loosely over her silent and sagging form- and her skin looks waxy and blue. She's long-blinking and empty-eyed, and though she stares in my direction, she seems not to see me. We sit in a now cold and darkening space- the embers having long since smoldered themselves dead- and the night's creeping darkness is held weakly at bay by the low-flickering flame of our candle's dripping nub.

It's a terrible feeling to be in the presence of a person in need of help you can't give, and that perfectly describes the situation here. As I look her over, it's clear to me that I showed up this morning for the day's escapade accidentally much better prepared than Chrissy. While we're both wearing weatherproof boots, knit caps, and passable hiking pants, the first obvious differentiator is our choice of handwear. Which is to say, I have gloves, and Chrissy does not. Why she didn't bring any is a moot point now, but it might very well end up costing her her fingers. Even more crucial, though, is our respective choice of coat- and here is where my luck kicked in. Chrissy is wearing a light and form-hugging jacket- perfectly appropriate for a day hike where you want to look adorable for your crush, but dangerously ill-conceived when seeking protection from a life-threatening blizzard. I, on the other hand, am wearing a chunky, hooded parka- and not by choice. Like Chrissy, I too set out this morning with my mind on fashion-over-function, but had to grudgingly leave my cute coat at home when I covered it in coffee on my way out the door. Cursing my bad luck, I was forced to grab Plan B: my winter anorak. Again, perfect universal alignment. Though maybe not for Chrissy.

Don't go thinking just because I'm wearing a heavier layer than my companion's windbreaker that I'm sufficiently insulated from this frozen deluge that seeks to swallow the cabin and all within. My plight is but a half-notch off Chrissy's. Despite my gloves and boots, I've gone numb in my extremities and I'm starting to feel a little foggy myself. I can still hold the blanket around me, but the meager warmth it spares won't suffice for much longer. As Night steals in through the cabin's chinks and gaps, I can feel its comrade- Cold- accompanying. Yes, this situation is on a sinister slide. As I take in our hibernal scene, a degenerate notion insinuates itself, engendered- no doubt- by the devil that lurks within us all. "No," my waning humanity replies, "I can't." (not yet)

I don't know how much good the story is doing Chrissy, but it's providing welcome diversion for me, so I shrug off my swelling stupor, and resume...

****

"It's trials you like, so it's trials you get," boomed Freyr over the terror-trembled forms of his cowering daughters. "You've played loose with lives, and now you'll know the price," continued the king. "I command you travel to the heart of the Cosmos, where you will find at its center the Tree of Life: the mighty Yggdrasil. From it you will pluck one leaf- no more, no less- then return to the base of Nur and drop it into the sea near the village you destroyed. Should Fortune favor, the lives you took will be restored. But take heed: if you fail me, your fate will be severe.

Do this now- and GO!" thundered the Immortal. Much relieved by this simple task, the sisters thanked their father for his grace and departed. Freyr but nodded grimly at their going, for he knew what lie in wait.

Across all space and time flew the sisters, until they arrived at the center of Being, and found there the walled Garden of Urd and its impenetrable jeweled gates. Defending the entry and the mystic garth within, was the tree giant, Nidhogg- Keeper of Yggdrasil. "State your quest," growled the sentry, who stood 200 meters tall, and had eyes that glowed with mercuric swirl- like opaline orbs of molten silver. "We serve the will of our father- the mighty god-king Freyr...," answered Skadi, "...who bids us fetch a leaf from the holy tree, Yggdrasil, and return it to the shores of Nur." "And tell me, Little Princess...," spoke Nidhogg with a cruel smile, "...did your father share with you the price that such a prize commands?" "He did not, Gatekeeper," her wary reply.

At this the watchman's wicked grin widened, and he flipped his war ax playfully into the air- catching it by the handle- then threw his head back, laughing with omen. "Well, Sisters..," he spoke as his smile faded, "...it appears your father has played a joke that only one of you will get." His eyes showed no humor at these words. "The tree does not surrender its leaves with volition, and so you must make recompense if you wish to reap its reward," continued the guardian. "And what compensation does the tree command, Steward?" queried Astrid with growing unease, for she feared the answer at which she silently guessed. "A life for a life, Your Highness," replied the giant. "And not done gently, either," he added with a sneer. "For as you rip from the tree the leaf you seek, so too must the life you give be ripped from its host." And now the sisters paled- for they saw clearly the consequence of their father's sanction: they were to duel one another- not just for the leaf- but also for their lives. Nidhogg saw the growing horror in the sisters' eyes, and his smile returned. "I see you now see..," he mocked, "...so gird yourselves and prepare your magic, for battle is upon you."

With these words, Nidhogg stepped aside and the mighty gates of Urd opened, revealing the Tree of Life and its shimmering verdure. "And now, Daughters of Freyr, let Yggdrasil reveal the stronger sister, then carry and keep her, and grant a sacred leaf as her reward." The sisters squared to face each other, their magic at the ready. And though their cheeks were tear-wet, their eyes were hard. "Ready!" spoke the treekeeper, "Fight!"

****

A coughing fit disrupts my narrative here, as I hunch over, retching myself dizzy. The coughing devolves to a hacking choke, but eventually subsides, and I struggle to straighten back up. My insensate fingers fail me, and the blanket slips off my shoulders- puddling around my numb and criss-crossed legs. I look to Chrissy and am not surprised to see her slumped over to the side, eyes closed, and blanket akimbo. The obscene voice returns- and this time I listen.

Shakily, I gain my feet and shuffle over to Chrissy for a closer look. But for the rasping wheeze that labors from her, she makes no sound. I remove a glove and lay the back of my hand to her cheek. She's ice cold and her flesh has the feel of hard plastic. At my touch, her blue lids flutter then open weakly, and she registers my presence in a moment of fleeting recognition. "Help," she mewls feebly.

Despite my own weakness, I manage to sit her upright, leaning her against the wall and stretching her legs out before her. She's dead weight, but has regained a modicum of consciousness and is able to follow my movements. I rearrange the knit cap onto her head, pulling it down over her ears and low across her forehead, and her dim-lit eyes reflect her gratitude. I next replace my glove, and reach for the blanket that's fallen off her shoulders. I meet her eyes, and ever so faintly, they glow with hope. I move toward her with the blanket and the whisper of a smile shapes her lips. Then- in a wide arc- I swing the blanket around and over my own shoulders, and her smile disappears. Our eyes meet and I see she knows my design. I start to turn away, but stop- a thought freezing me in place. I wheel back toward her as a begging squeal escapes her- that I ignore. Then, in a single movement, I swipe the cap off her head and turn from her again. And this time for good.

****

Blaire Blake had the blues

Blaire Blake had the blues. She had the blues mostly because she felt bad for the world and didn't know what to do about helping it get the help it needed. And she knew so much about the world and the help it needed because every time she turned around, it seemed someone was showing her a picture or telling her a story about the bad things that were happening everywhere all about. And she heard just as much about the bad things that were happening far away, too. Seemed everywhere she looked Blaire saw pain.

And what pain did Blaire see? Well the obvious, of course; the same things those who have looked have found since for time always: war, famine, poverty, mistreatment, indifference, et cetera et cetera. But Blaire had a unique eye for detail, too, so she also saw pain in places many overlooked. For example, she saw things in people's eyes- things they thought they were hiding, but not from Blaire. So Blaire saw all the pain the world was trying to show her, plus much of the pain the world wanted to hide from her, too. And it all made her feel lonely and unprepared.

Because that's another thing- Blaire also felt destitute. That's not to say that she was destitute. It's not like she was that refugee holding a baby in a muddy crater in some wartorn hellscape on the evening news. Her sense of destitution was due mostly to being constantly reminded of what she didn't have: the cars, the clothes, the houses, the boys. It wasn't the being without that got to her, so much as the always being told she was without that ground her down. But she did live hand-to-mouth off her modest sales clerk salary, and it was true she had no money to protect herself if she got sick, and her boyfriend Chase did run off with someone recently, and on and on. So it's not like she didn't have grievances, but it's all relative, you know? Try telling someone who is hurting to look on the bright side because they could always be hurting worse, and see where that gets you, though.

Yes, Blaire Blake had the blues.

Now when you have the blues, you do a lot of sitting around, considering your options. Your options on how to get yourself out of the blues, that is. At least that's what Blaire did. And by process of elimination, Blaire eventually determined that her best course of action- and the thing she would do next in order to kick the blues- was to become a school teacher. As in, get off the sofa and put her degree to work, help some kids, maybe make some new friends- it seemed a logical fit. So that's what she did. And after eight weeks of completing forms and taking electronic courses, the powers-that-be saw fit not only to certify Blaire a bona fide high school History teacher, but also to drop her into a real-life classroom, posthaste.

At the start Blaire was quite pleased with her new state of affairs: fresh faces, young minds, summers off- it looked like this was going to be just the distraction she needed. Good-bye, blues! Or so Blaire thought. It turned out though, that Blaire's feelings of energized excitement were short-lived, as was the honeymoon phase of her new career. For it wasn't a semester into the new school year before Blaire began to comprehend a problematic truth: turns out she hated kids. Or more specifically: she hated teenagers. Or more specifically still: Blaire hated the teenagers she was assigned to teach. Every single one of them. Couldn't stand them. And as one might imagine, this made for a less-than-optimal work environment.

Part of her disdain Blaire came by naturally. Teenagers are, after all, rather unrelenting in their sarcasm, their general self-absorption, and their indifference to authority. And for the unprepared, this can be quite a shock. Also, when it comes to snark, teenagers are downright vicious, especially if they smell blood in the water, as they did with newbie Blaire. Having grown up an only child and not having kids herself, Blaire was caught on the hop by the peccadilloes and far-ranging hormonal vicissitudes of the teenage set. And it was this unique combination of ingénue and teen scorn that tilled the soil for a contentious and angst-ridden station.

To be fair, though, this was hardly the fault of the students. These were just kids being kids. Even the bad ones- of which there were only one or two- weren't that bad. A foul word here, a banned item there- that was about it. By nearly any teacher's measure, this was a well-behaved group of youths. Enviably so. In truth, the friction between student and teacher had much more to do with Blaire than anything else. For in addition to being impatient with the learning process (any forgotten date, misremembered battle, or improperly ordered dynasty was sure to send Ms. Blake into a silent, death-staring fury), Blaire was also humorless and ceaselessly condescending to her class, and this made her no friends. Had she any modicum of experience, Blaire would have known that nothing sets a teenager against you faster than dismissing their voice. And it was Blaire's steady state to wholesale disregard nearly everything her students thought and said about anything that mattered to them. A fact not lost on the kids.

But despite the odium that swirled within Blaire's classroom, she did an admirable job of keeping her cool, and she worked hard to retain the bearing and stature of a dour-though-unfailingly-professional Educator. She pursued this reputation with single minded intent, because she needed above all else to be above all reproach. She needed this spotless reputation for cover. Because Blaire Blake had a secret. Two secrets, really.

Blaire's first secret was that she had a mean streak. Maybe it was only-child entitlement, maybe it was pre-spinster anxiety, maybe it was just wiring. However engendered, Blaire hated to be contradicted, she hated to be second-guessed, and above all, she hated to lose. And every time she stepped into that classroom, Blaire felt like she was losing to these sniggering, eye-rolling brats. And that just wouldn't do. In fact, it was a situation that required action.

Blaire's second secret was that every night when she went home- after another infuriating day of butting heads and biting tongues- she changed into sweats, drew the shades, grabbed a glass of wine, and sat down in front of her computer, where she would spend the rest of the evening- and even sometimes into the early morning, "soul bowling," as she gleefully called it. In other words, Blaire Blake was a troll.

It was a pretty straightforward enterprise: sow discord and mistrust amongst the school's teenaged ranks by way of a randomly-targeted, completely anonymous, and unrelenting misinformation campaign. There are models for how to do this all over the place. Deep state and special interest operatives have been attacking the opposition's collective psyche ever since there were shadows and snakes to do it. So Blaire just took a page out of their book. And after much study, she distilled her recipe for creating chaos down to a 3-step process: rumor torrent, false concern, and contextual misdirection. Here's how it went:

Blaire's first stop on any new "cry campaign" (her snide moniker) was always the teachers' lounge: the school's best source of gossip and tattle. It's here she shopped for targets. Because unbeknownst to the kids, the teachers- who may have seemed like they weren't paying attention- almost always were. And while Blaire wasn't well-liked, or a source of advice and guidance for the kids, many of the other teachers often served the role of student confidant. And these same well-meaning instructors were prone to labor under the misimpression that all members of their profession share their compassion and concern for student well-being. As a result, they in turn regularly sought counsel from their colleagues on matters of teenage adversity and woe. And Blaire, The Stiff-But-Fair, was among this advisory cast, which meant her intel game was strong.

After mining the teachers' lounge for the drama du jour, Blaire would select her hapless quarry and move into the first phase of her offensive: rumor torrent. Using a fake identity (and Blaire had many- they're easy to come by, if you know where to look), she'd build a web of "they said/ I heards" that she'd spin across the various boards and forums that comprised the school's social epicenter. Like setting a spark to dry tinder, it took very little to spread the blaze of hearsay around and about. And once this mist of innuendo had been spritzed across the rumor-hungry student body, Blaire would implement the second phase of her attack: feigned concern.

Again using a variety of fake names and profiles, Blaire would bestrew the web with a bevy of anonymous well-wishes aimed at the very target of her antipathy. All of them insincere, and all of them meant to insinuate doubt where there was none before: "Hey Y'all, just asking you to join me in keeping an eye on Joanie. She's such a sweet girl, and

I hate to see her struggling with her weight. You're beautiful, Girl- just keep being you!" Or, "CTA Everyone- I'm worried about Jimmy. I know he's been down lately, and I just want everyone to join me in letting him know it will be alright. Everyone has down days, Jimmy- please don't do anything drastic. We're in this together- PNL! :-)" It was amazing how well these tricks set the tongues to wagging.

Once the rumors were whispered and the mistruths implied, things were left for a bit and the garden was let to grow. During this time, Blaire kept close watch on her prey, paying particular attention to the children's tell-all eyes, and the growing hurt they secretly revealed to her. When the pain was at its fever pitch and the rumors had done their work, only then would Blaire swing her final stroke: false context. In Blaire's experience, nothing pushes the tender teen over the edge quite as effectively as irrefutable truth presented in a false light.

Doctor appointments took on new meaning when coupled with rumors that Joanie was recently seen perusing the family planning aisle at the local pharmacy. Eyebrows were raised at the news Jimmy was seen buying a length of rope at the hardware store, particularly given the whispers of his bathroom crying sessions. Never mind that Joanie was at an orthodontist appointment, and never mind that Jimmy's mom asked him to get materials for her crafting closet- truth always lost sway to suspicion when placed in the context of fib and fiction.

And this went on for months. In fact, according to the playbook on psychological warfare, it's meant to take a while; the longer the slice, the deeper the cut. Misinformation sprinkled about in random and arbitrary patterns, nearly impossible to trace back to an always-moving source. Blaire delighted in it. She loved seeing the sidelong glances being tossed around her classroom. She loved seeing the kids sending surreptitious messages around the room. She loved the malicious whisper-giggles she heard when her back was turned. And while she came down on the kids for all of it- and hard, too- she loved every bit and every moment.

Yes, it seemed Blaire Blake had finally kicked the blues.

So there she was one night, sitting in her comfies, three glasses deep, giggling at her own clever malevolence, when a staccato rap on the door rattled Blaire from her reverie. No one ever knocked on her door- like ever- so this was something new. Blaire grudgingly rose from her seat and made her way to the front entry, which she opened in a state of mild annoyance to find standing there... nothing, no one; her stoop was empty. Some jerk kid, probably- Blaire growled inwardly to herself- then made to shut the door and return to her project, when an object on the front mat caught her eye.

It was a buff-colored manila envelope, the kind with the little string on the flap that you figure-eight between two nubs to close. Across the front of it was written a single word: liar. It was written in cursive. Blaire looked around hoping to find the messenger, but the street all about was silent. Confusedly, she shut the door and retreated to her curtained chamber, where under the harsh glow of the bare-bulbed entry light she unwound the envelope's thread, reached beneath its flap, then withdrew and read the contents.

After a few moments of rigid silence, a letter dropped distractedly from Blaire's hands.

****

Ms. Blake thought she was getting away clean, but Felix Howe was onto her. Because while Felix may have swung to the slight side of average in nearly every category that teenagers are told matters to them, he's nobody's fool. And once he started paying attention, Felix realized that Ms. Blake was the troll who was targeting his best friend, Jimmy DiFalco. And this would not do. In fact, it was a situation that required action.

His first indication that something was off was when he started hearing rumors that Jimmy was feeling down and might want to hurt himself. Nothing could have been further from the truth. Jimmy and Felix were best friends going all the way back to first grade; ever since the DiFalcos moved from Providence into the house next door to Felix and his mom. If something had been off with Jimmy, Felix would have known it. So his intuition was already humming. But what really put Felix's ears up was the encounter he and Jimmy had with Ms. Blake at the hardware store, a month or so after rumors of Jimmy's distress started flowing.

Mrs. DiFalco had asked the boys to get her a skein of yellow slub yarn (whatever that was) for a knitting project she was working on. So Jimmy and Felix had made their way over to the craft aisle at Nelson's and were perusing the options, when who should wander around the corner but everyone's least favorite teacher, Ms. Blake, of freshman History infamy. The two parties exchanged somber greetings, then the boys grabbed a roll of yarn and got out of there as quickly as possible. But for Ms. Blake and the checkout kid, Felix and Jimmy had been the only ones in the store. Felix was sure of it. They had scoured every aisle of that place looking for a 'skein' of anything, before the unfortunate crossing with Ms. Blake. And so when the lie was passed around that Jimmy had been at the hardware store shopping for rope, Felix immediately knew where to start his hunt.

It took about a week for Felix to connect Ms. Blake to her stable of puppet nom de guerres: *VarsityBlu, CougarPrideGrl, Scrillaz2122,* and *NeverBeenKissed420*. It's not like Felix was some sort of genius hacker- his computer skills were middling, at best- it's just that Ms. Blake's attempts to hide her identity were so laughably inadequate. It's like she was bringing a floppy disk to a gunfight. In fairness, she covered her tracks pretty well for someone her age, but you'd better know your way around a computer- and good- if you're going to play war games with teenagers. Felix tracked her down in a hot minute. And then he waited and watched.

And what he heard and saw infuriated him. Not so much for Jimmy's sake- Jimmy couldn't have cared less about the limp rumors floating around on him. He was even borderline amused by it all. No, Jimmy was just fine. Felix's anger and indignation were aroused instead on behalf of Joanie Chisholm, the cute quiet girl who sat in front of him in Pre-Algebra, and the object of Felix's crushing affection. It was obvious to anyone watching- and especially to Felix- that Joanie was not ok with the cruel implications and lies being whispered about her. She wasn't doing well in the face of the teen judgments being hurled her way from every quarter. Joanie wasn't fine at all. Her eyes showed it, and Felix saw it. And it all made him very angry.

Now when a person makes you really angry, sometimes it's good to turn the other cheek; to be the bigger individual and embrace peaceful resistance. And sometimes the only thing that makes a fella feel better when he's feeling mad is 'git back.' And that's just the path that Felix chose. So it was in this spirit of retributive justice- after a week of reflection and preparation- that Felix sat down at the kitchen table and in his best handwriting penned the following letter:

Dear Ms. Blake,

I know you've been trolling kids at school, and I know the 4 different aliases you use. So let's not play. I'm not writing to tell you I know. I'm writing to tell you what I did about it. My first thought when I figured out it was you was I should turn you in and get you fired. But I was afraid they might just give you a warning or something. And that didn't seem fair. I also figured even if they did fire you, you'd probably just keep trolling other kids somewhere else anyways. So I kept thinking. My second thought was that maybe I'd troll you back. Steal your credit card number or social security number or something and mess with your credit or something. But I don't know how to do that, plus you're not worth getting in trouble for. So then I decided that I'd ask my Uncle Mike for advice. He's not really my uncle. We're not even related. But I've known him since I was a little kid and he always looks out for me and my mom. So I asked him what he thought I should do. And he told me I should write you this letter. He said in the letter I should tell you that before he moved to Arizona, he lived in Rhode Island, and that when he lived in Rhode Island he was in the news a lot. He said to tell you you should look him up and see. He also said to remind you that every single one of those charges was dropped. The violent ones too. He also wanted me to tell you that trolling is bad and that you shouldn't do it and that he wants to talk to you about it right away. He said to tell you if you don't call him in the next 10 minutes that some people will call on you instead. He said to make extra sure to let you know you shouldn't let that happen. He was really adamant about it. Then he told me to tell you to call him at (600) 653-2761. He said to tell you to ask for Michael DiFalco. So that's what I did when I found out it was you.

Sincerely,
Felix Howe

After Felix finished writing his letter, he dropped it in an envelope and he and Jimmy rode their bikes to the address Uncle Mike had gotten for him. Next, the friends put the note on their teacher's porch, banged on her door, then ran across the street to watch from behind a tree.

And just like that, Blaire Blake's blues were back.

****

1000 words

100
Ever consider that perhaps all this moral decay is actually human evolution in disguise? That in truth, Ethics impedes social progress? Maybe "me" is more important than "we", today does trump tomorrow, and might does make right. After all, but for war we wouldn't enjoy half the modern conveniences we do: jet engines, preservatives, zippers. Heck, we wouldn't even have satellite television. So I say forget your neighbor, keep looking out for Number One. Steal. Lie. Cheat. And thanks. Because Mankind stands only to gain from these multitudinous shenanigans and tomfooleries of ours. (Though admittedly, I could have it wrong.)

200
I am here to tell you that magic is real. You can hardly be blamed for not believing; yours is an epoch of babel and din- conditions ill suited to seeing that which logic commands one to dismiss. Most magic anymore has gone to deep disguise; to find it you must seek its sanctuary: places of profound stillness and gentle light. Sunrise on the open sea, moonglow in the desert, high long views down open valleys- these are good places to search. Yes magic still abounds; it waits in silence for a later age- one yet friendlier to its delights.

300
I've heard it said that History defines us by moments, and it got me wondering if maybe we don't define ourselves by moments, too. I'd like to think those few kindnesses I did tell my tale, but I know better. Because I'm in on all the other stuff: those myriad untold cruelties, omissions, and lies. I know what's off record, Senator- so to speak. So when the past amount comes due, keep your fingers crossed that we're just a name on some list- a box to be checked- rather than a specimen to be dissected, and every truth thereby revealed.

400
Time is short, so pay close attention. I have a message for you from the Opposed. They're pleased with your performance and want you to keep doing what you're doing. Indignation, feigned commitment, insincere references to long neglected principles; you're a master of the craft and one of the best we have. When this is all over, there's a great spot waiting for you amongst the faceless masses. You're gonna love it, everyone has it exactly the same. I have to go now- the hunters are always on my heels. Have faith and remember: capitulation is key to our success.

500
My research suggests that to look important it's important to wear suspenders- extra points for braces- and strictly no jacket. Pay attention if you doubt me. Suspenders are the thing; cufflinks, too. If you're a lady, keep that pantsuit handy- you'll probably land a big deal if you wear it. I guess the thing is- from pauper to president- everyone has a uniform. Unfortunately for me, few boardroom deals happen in flip flops. I hold out hope though that someday jeans and tshirts will be as ubiquitous at the conference table as pocket squares. Everyone wants to look important, right?

600
Once there was a man who discovered a great secret about how it all works. But in trying to explain what that secret is, the man was greatly confused. It's not the kind of secret one can tell another person, he realized. It can't be spoken aloud- that's not the way. This is the kind of secret that can only be passed by crucible. That is, wisdom as the wage of experience gained by test. Wisdom that is earned, not granted. And the man knew that grasping what this means, means everything. So he set himself out to understand it.

700
I have some good coals glowing tonight and my mind starts thinking: there's no need to always fuss the fire, to always be poking at it. The best ones you light right, and burn long. It's fun to stoke a fire, no doubt- to see it blaze big. But your wood goes fast that way; and fire is life in the wild. Real masters of camp burn mellow and settle in. Take time to get her going, then keep her going all night. You treat a great fire like you treat your favorite lover, and stay for a perfect while.

800
What of us will be unearthed a million years hence? Some plastic gewgaw, fossils of their ancestors, the unintelligible silhouette of a long past and crumbled place, perhaps? Or maybe there won't even be anything nor anyone around to dig upon this wet green rock, and everything will simply slide back to stillness. Then this mote against a pinhead of light that we call 'here' will keep to drift silently onward, hurtling along through the black nothing- toward infinitely more nothing- waiting on the Whole for to be reabsorbed. So that each and everything all can once again be one.

900
I sleep but little, and dream but much. I have but wants, and need but nots. I drown by drops, I madden by grains. This place, my part: they go on grace. I gather the wool, I give the gold. I lead the three, I feed the four. In balance this life; a gift gone goes when death is come. I fear no light, for faith is near. Then welcome the dark, as day is done. The nows go quick; quick come the stops. I sleep but little, and think but much. I madden by grains and drown by drops.

1000
Dear Jack: Such a delight to see you at the Admiral's clambake last weekend. Our conversation hasn't left my mind for five minutes since! I was thinking and giggling on your downright ribald impersonation of Bernice, when it occurred to me that some people leave destruction in their wake. They leave things worse than they found them. They don't destroy with intention. (do they?) Counterintuitively, they often live with great compassion. Too much compassion perhaps. Their empathies consume them. And rather than light the fuze of change, their flame sets fire to the brush. Love to Susan. Sincerely, Ms. Peacock

****

everyone dies of something

Everyone dies of something, so Max used to tell me- right up until the time when his heart and liver imploded in synchronicity. He'd say it by way of toast, lifting his see-through toward me with a nod as he blew cigarette smoke out his nose like a paunchy, middle-aged dragon. I used to think the sentiment was a defense mechanism against his fear of the beyond; a steeling self-affirmation steeped in grim acknowledgement of his vices and their unavoidable consequence. Now I think maybe he just didn't give a damn, and was smirking alongside the Reaper at that inside joke only the reckless understand: you can't run from it, so you'd might as well dance toward it. I want another drink. It's 9:45am.

Max was what's known in the business as a Cleaner; an assassin brought in by ownership to get rid of that which cannot be gotten rid of. We met on a job in Portland; it was an impossible Monday in late February: wet, icy, and gray. The kind of day where no one comes around. I had just finished scraping the windshields, and was making my way back to the portable-cum-office for a reheated cup of yesterday's coffee. I stomped the slush off myself and went in to find Maurice talking to a guy in a black Macintosh and wet Hush Puppies.

"This is Max," he said without preamble, "he's here to move the metal you losers can't sell. Show him around the lot and do what he says. He's in charge 'til he leaves." Max offered me a silky smooth hand, a wide, tobacco-stained grin, and a slap on the back. "Pleased to meet you, I'm Max!" he bubbled, a little too ebulliently. "Thanks for your time, I know you're busy!" (I wasn't.) "I'd sure appreciate a tour of your lovely site on this lovely day. If you don't mind, let's start with the pigs." With that, he launched himself out the door and into the sleet, me trudging after.

We spent the next two hours reviewing the lot's modest collection of junkers and jalopies, starting- as Max had requested- with the most unsellable first, moving up the ladder from there, and eventually making our way to the least undesirable of our uninspired inventory. He knew his stuff ("You boys got a good upholstery guy, that flood damage is well-hidden...") and asked only statements ("This lady's seen some action, bent frame and all, eh?") By tour's end, he knew the lineup as well as anyone on the team, and said to me with another smiling slap on the back, "I think I got it, Jack- thanks for the time. Ain't no one coming out in this weather though, so we'll sell these beasts tomorrow. Now let's get drunk." I couldn't argue with that- Max was boss now.

What ensued was the first of ten years' worth of drunken bull sessions with a man trench-wizened in that unique way only a lifelong salesman can be. His sagacity was wide-ranging, covering such varied topics as psychology ("No one buys from a guy they don't like..."), politics ("Some go into the game for the right reasons, they all stay for the wrong ones..."), relationships ("Love hurts but loneliness kills..."), money ("Might be the root of all evil, but poverty don't put pudding on your plate..."), life ("Forget the past- you can't regret what you don't remember..."), and, of course, death. In addition to his barroom wisdom, Max also taught me the indelicate craft of Cleaning.

After spending a week selling nearly every car on our lot, Max received his cut and took back to the road. On his way out the door, he grabbed me by the lapels and brought me with him. Must have liked the cut of my jib. Or maybe he just wanted a drinking buddy who listened more than he talked. Whatever his motivation, Max- my dead drunk sensei- taught me to seek the thrill of closing the unsellable sale. Speaking of which...

About a month ago I came into an opportunity I couldn't pass up. Goes like this: an upstart group of guttersnipes out of Provo had decided to take a swing for the fences in the highly lucrative- and very competitive- world of snack foods; specifically, potato chips. These guys had been watching the big boys experiment with exotic flavors for a few years, and they felt they could grab a piece of the action before anyone noticed. So they toyed around in the kitchen and came up with a few flavors. They floated a thousand units of peanut butter and jelly kettle chips to the Salt Lake market and sold out nearly overnight. Feeling pretty good about themselves, they followed up with another 5,000 units of PB&J, plus 2,500 of Moscow Mule. Same thing, immediate sell-out. At this point, they were thinking they had the game figured out and went in heavy: 10,000 units of PB&J, 10,000 units of Moscow Mule, regional distribution to three states, and- just for yucks- 5,000 units of their newest flavor: Blackened Tilapia. The first two SKUs continued to sell well, but Tilapia was a dud and it threatened to sink the whole ship. They tried discounting through their retailers, but no dice. One of the long poles in the snack food tent is product expiration, and these fellas were running up against it. They had six months to move their inventory before their dates went bad, and that's where I came in. Cleaners often run lines in a few different channels. In addition to cars, paper products, and children's textiles, I dabble in snack foods. So when these guys started looking for serious help, word got to me and I reached out. Long story short, I offered them a deal that made their problems a little smaller and provided a handsome success fee for me. Which is why I sit here now in the middle of nowhere Utah with a sour gut and a truckload full of snacks that taste like cajun-spiced bass bait, waiting to meet with the proprietress of Margot's Curios Cave. There's a slight tremble in my left hand. I could really go for that drink. 9:56.

As I stand here in the empty store (the sales clerk wandered outside 20 minutes ago to find Margot) I'm spellbound by my bizarre surroundings. Self-styled as, "The World's Worst Gift Shop," they don't give one much to argue with. And they aren't calling this a cave for kitsch- it's literally in a cave. Deep and dark- all damp and no sizzle. Light comes from fluorescent bars mounted against the slimy walls and powered, I assume, by an out-of-sight generator. The air mopes sluggishly about with a nudge from an oscillating fan set on the floor against the cave's east wall. The shop's wares are displayed on a harlequin patchwork of busted up steel shelving, jury-rigged cinder blocks and two-by-eights, and mildewed wooden bookshelves. The smell is fecund and I'm pretty sure I just saw a bat. There's a distinct vibe given off here of a serial killer's unfinished basement. And then there's the inventory.

I'm not for certain, but it appears that at least half of everything in here is broken, damaged, or partially-eaten. That's not a joke. In the 'Bargain Bin' (which is a sawed-off oil drum) I'm looking right now at an opened bag of Raul's Tamarind Crunch Wafers ($1.99). I happen to know Raul's SnackCo was shut down two years ago due to a catalog of well-publicized and well-deserved health code violations. Along the west wall, there's an entire display of broken dream catchers ("the perfect gift for that not-so-special someone who's hope you want to kill"), and in the 'Clothing Corner' there are novelty t-shirts and hats from at least 10 different tourist destinations- none of them the Curios Cave. That's just a sampling- the shop is a menagerie of chaos that defies explanation. I've seen some stuff in my time, but I've never wandered into an asylum like this. I can't wait to meet Margot. It's 10am sharp. And here she is.

It's hard to tell if she's good-looking or not. I mean, she's definitely not now, but she might have been at one point. She's tough to pin because she has the trappings of once-ago beauty (a dancer's lithe physique, well-styled blond hair falling just below the shoulder, laughing and luminous green eyes) and the face of a catcher's mitt that's been crosshatched and leathered by too much sun in youth. Multiple scarred-over piercings in her nose and ears suggest wilder days of an earlier age, and hints of ink peek out at her cuffs betraying tat sleeves under her form-hugging leather jacket. She wears tight jeans and roughed up cowboy boots; no makeup, no jewelry. She moves with confidence and grace, coming toward me with her hand held out warmly, and a white, slightly gapped smile. I place her age somewhere between 30 and 80, with the over-under on the downslide of 50. While far from beautiful, she has unconventional sex appeal, and I'm surprisingly smitten.

"Hi Jack, I'm Margot, welcome to my freaky little outpost," she says with an endearing giggle. "Can I get you something to drink? There's water or tea. Or if you're feeling funky..." she adds with a wink, "...I can get you a soda from the world's worst snack bar. We have strawberry meatloaf cola, maple bacon seltzer, and wasabi root beer. I'd avoid the coffee (smile)- it's worse than the soda."

"I'm ok for now, thank you, but maybe I'll try the meatloaf later- I did skip breakfast." Max always said there's a fine line between flirt and charm, and the key to a good sale is tiptoeing along it. "Ok, well let me know... How about a tour of the grounds before we start talking taters? You can help me feed the peacock." I have no idea what she's talking about, but I'll bite. "Sure...," I say with a grin, "...lead the way."

She takes me through the front door of the walled-in cave, which appears (earmuffs, Fire Marshal) to be the only way in or out. From there we go through the parking lot and around to the right of the shop where- hidden from roadside view- there's a small meadow abutting the hill into which the cave is bored. In the meadow is parked a dilapidated trailer with a handwritten poster board reading, "World's Worst Snack Bar." It's here, I presume, where one might sample such delights as meatloaf soda and only-God-knows what else. Behind the trailer is a slapdash aviary of chicken wire and telephone poles, housing- one further presumes- at least a peacock. There are also a couple of picnic tables splashed around the grassy space, as well as a weed-choked horseshoe pit. A sun-faded port-a-potty hides behind a tree. In the far corner of the meadow is a broken down and rusted-out tractor. Thrown haphazardly over the gearshift is a sign that reads, "Tetanus Tony says: play at your own risk!" The meadow scene does nothing to offset the disorienting insanity of the cave shop, but I grudgingly admit, this place has a madman's appeal; something about the devil-may-care attitude of it all. It reveals something about Margot and her bohemian spirit. Not sure what my attraction to it all reveals about me.

Margot pops her head into the snack trailer and comes out with a plastic bag of moldy hamburger buns that she hands to me as she moves toward the aviary, clearly intending for me to follow. "For Mr. Bird...," she says over her shoulder. She holds the chicken wire door open for me as we proceed to tear up the buns and sprinkle them around for the cage's single occupant, Mr. Bird: a beautiful beast of blue and green plumage with the talons of a raptor, who seems uninterested in our presence. We leave him to peck lazily at the lackluster fare, and take up seats at the picnic table nearest the cage. It's a perfect spring morning with a golden sun glowing down bright from a blue and fat-clouded sky. Margot speaks first.

"This usually goes one of two ways. Most people wander around looking slightly confused, mumble something polite, and hit the road as quickly as possible. But some...," she smiles at me with those sparkling green eyes, "...are strangely enchanted by it all and linger for a closer look. Where do you fall out, Jack?" It's not a defiant or challenging question, and I have the impression my answer will in no way affect our business dealings. She's simply trying to figure out where I land on the scale of oddity. "I've never seen anything like it before, Margot," I say truthfully. "I like it." To my surprise, I realize this, too, is the truth.

She searches my eyes for a moment at this answer, then perks with a widening grin, "Yeah, me too. It was a gift from my ex-husband. *Third* ex-husband," she adds with a smile. "It ended the only way a good marriage can- he died." "I'm sorry to hear that." "Don't be. Like I said, it's the best elegant exit if you want to end things friendly-like. Any exes on your ledger, Jack?" "Two." "Any dead ones?" "Nope. Both alive and kicking. And scratching. And biting." "Well we can't all be so lucky," she giggles, then continues, "...anyhow, when Grayson died he left me the deed to 12 acres in southern Utah. I had never even been to Utah before and, to my knowledge, neither had Gray. But he knew my fascination with caves, so he found one and bought it for me. He was cool like that." She pauses for a moment in sweet remembrance. "I had no interest in Utah- I was an LA girl, born and raised. But out of morbid curiosity I came to check the place out. It spoke to me in a weird way and I accidentally fell in love with it here." "Ah, love," I say. "Ah, love...," she echoes with a smile. "I decided to turn the place into a roadside attraction and stay for a while. I figured if I was going to do it, I'd might as well do it weird, so I went around to a bunch of thrift stores, bought the craziest stuff I could find, and 'The World's Worst Gift Shop' was born. That was 5 years ago now. About 2 years ago, I took on the same model and created the 'World's Worst Snack Bar.' Instead of thrift shops, I get my inventory from manufacturers looking to get rid of discontinued lines and flavors. I don't have to tell you, there's some gross stuff out there. That's Margot's Cave in a nutshell. What's your excuse for being here, Jack?"

Sharing a story is always part of the sale. It's how you break the ice and create connection. Max used to say keep it broad and self-deprecating, lightly personal, and never anything political or religious. Even if you get a read on the other's views, steer clear or you'll be dragged away from the ultimate goal: the close. Self-deprecating is good because it shows you don't take yourself too seriously. People like that. My left hand is really starting to shake now- I hide it in my lap.

"My story's not exactly Hollywood material. I was raised in Oregon, joined the army after high school, spent 4 years in Germany, moved back to Portland after the service and got a job selling kid's shoes at Castleman's department store. I hated the product, but liked sales, so I went in search of new peaks to conquer. I tried on used cars, then paper milling, then wholesale fabrics, before moving into the big leagues." "Potato chips?" she asks smilingly. "Potato chips," I smile back. "Managed to pick up a couple of ex-wives along the way. Lost the dog both times in the divorce. I also have a son who's grown and lives in Spokane. Then I came to Margot's Curios Cave. The end." "I don't know, Jack, that sounds like a movie I'd watch." "Your bar is low." Friendly smiles exchanged.

Max always told me there are three stages to every sale: education, deliberation, and decision, and they're bookended by rapport and close. If you haven't set the right mood, the middle three don't happen right. And even if everything else goes perfectly, if you don't know when to tie it all together, you'll never get to the finish line. It's time to start educating Ms. Margot on the finer points of fish-flavored potato treats. That left hand is really going now. I hazard a glance at my watch. 10:26. If we get this thing moving, I could be into that glove box by 11, 11:30 latest.

"So besides terrible soda, tell me more about the offerings at the 'World's Worst Snack Bar'," I entreat. "Do you sell any chips?" "Jack," Margot says teasingly, "...are you getting ready to invite me to the parking lot to show me what's in the back of your truck?" "I, uh..."

"Kidding, kidding. Hey, I'll make it easy. To be honest, blackened tilapia chips sound disgusting and I have no interest in tasting them. I do, however, have a huge interest in selling them. I suspect they will immediately jump into second place as the worst thing on the menu- just behind strawberry meatloaf soda. So I'll make you a deal. I'll take all of them off your hands on one condition: you have to let me read your palm. I know that sounds crazy, but here's my dilemma. Palm reading is my newest hobby and I want to offer it as a service at the cave, but I don't have anyone to practice on besides Julie- who you met on the way in- and who's future is not that interesting. Frankly, according to her palm, it's pretty bleak. Don't tell her I said that, I've been trying to paint her a good picture." I smile. "Anyhow, if you let me do a reading, I'll take those terrible chips off your hands and you can start your weekend early. What do you say?" The glove box beckons and my hand shakes its approval. "How could I say 'no' to an offer like that?"

I hold my right hand out to her across the picnic table and she takes it into hers, which are supple and warm. She examines it closely- back to front- then motions for my left. I feel it trembling in my lap and it causes me to pause for half a blink before I shrug inwardly and pass it over, too. Similar to the right, she studies this one back to front, as well, tracing a slow finger over the lines and ridges of my quavering palm. Her finger lingers on the rippling surface as she looks up and into my eyes with a glimmer of understanding, holds for a beat, then drops her gaze back to my hands.

"Your heart is full of love," she begins. "You're a man of great aspiration, and though your ambition is large, you are humble and grateful for your many blessings. You are funny and charismatic; people like you and your life is rich with friends." As she speaks, her finger moves across the tracks of my shaking palm, connecting line to line in a deliberate and unbroken flow. Her eyes remain downward cast; her voice is low. "You travel wide, but you've never met a stranger. Your greatest strength is your lack of fear. Your life has been a grand adventure...," at this she looks up and meets my eyes, "... but your best is yet to come." To the last detail, everything she has just said is wrong. I hold her look, she holds my shaking hand.

"Amazing," I lie. "I'd say you have a bright future ahead of you as a gypsy." I don't have the stomach for truth right now. Her smile twists to a smirk, and I know she's unconvinced. "Sit tight, I'll be right back," she says and gives my hand a squeeze.

She disappears behind the snack trailer, returning a moment later with a bottle and two jelly jars that she plunks down on the picnic table as she retakes her seat. I must look surprised because her laugh is playful and self-conscious. I don't know what to say, so I say nothing. She sits silently for a moment, looking over my shoulder and across the meadow.

"You gotta love the universe," she says, halfway to herself, "...always with a trick up her sleeve." Still not sure where this is going, I hold my silence. "I'm not the sentimental type, but I did wake up this morning hoping for a distraction. Gray died six years ago today." I start to speak, but she stops me with a raised hand and meets my eye. "No need for that, I was just oversharing." She regains her smile, green eyes mischievously ablaze. "He lived hard and no one was surprised when he went out early. But I do like to remember him each year with a drink, and you strike me as the type who wouldn't mind joining." "I don't often turn down a drink," I admit, as I reach for the bottle and fill the jars strong, "...and never from a lady." Margot smiles at this and takes the jar I offer. "To Gray and the love of strange places," I say, lifting my drink to hers. She taps her glass to mine and smiles.

"To the art of the close," she adds with a wink.

****

know your friends

They say you know your friends by who shows up when it's time to move. If that's the case, I guess I'm Simon's only friend, or at least his best friend, seeing as how it was just the two of us there, laboring under the Phoenix sun, moving his stuff into the back of a hauler in August heat that was much too hot to be healthy. Evidently, some final straw had been broken the night before between him and Estrella, and he was decamping from their cohabitation unit ASAP.

Despite my early arrival the next morning, Estrella (Simon told me) was long gone, and we had all the time we needed to carry out our task without any fear of interruption. As so often happens in the near wake of a breakup, my friend was awash with a combination of anger, indignation, and bittersweet recall. This unique alchemy of emotions had a stupefying effect on him, resulting in a conversation that was punctuated by lots of far-off gazes and mid-sentence silences. It made for pretty lousy talk, so eventually we drifted into silence and I contented myself with my own imaginings.

I was inside the unit taking a break from the sun, and boxing the contents of some shelves Simon had pointed out as being his, when I came across a book- the only book, in fact- amongst his varied menagerie of knick knacks, bibelots, and minor awards. It was the title that caught my eye: Wisdom of the First Nuclear Age: 108 Fables for Children, by Talese Thumbwick. You could tell it was old by the pages- they were heavy polymer, not like the wispy sheets they roll out on books today. This thing was definitely vintage, probably late Second Nuclear Age, maybe older. As I thumbed through the decadent volume, enjoying its heft, I alighted upon the book's dog-eared introduction. Intrigued, I read:

Wisdom of the First Nuclear Age: 108 Fables for Children
Author's Preface, by Talese Thumbwick

Welcome, Reader! Throughout human existence, our race has sought to answer the question 'why?' that surrounds so many of our common life experiences: war, love, death, soul, birth, time, et cetera. And to answer these questions, many civilizations have relied on allegory and myth to provide a framework for their epoch's attempt at explanation. So was it with our ancient forebears of the First Nuclear Age (F.N.A.).

The fables and their lessons that follow may seem equal parts foreign and familiar to you. This is to be expected. The tales seem foreign because they are old. Very old. Keep in mind, these stories were written and handed down by tribes that lived just prior to the Great Self-Slaughter, over 1,000 years ago! For that reason, some of the cultural mores expressed- particularly the seeming infatuation with individuality and personal choice- will likely come across as misguided at best, and barbaric at worst. You may find it helpful when you encounter one of these social eccentricities to think of them more as moral fossils suitable for excavation and study, rather than modern-day guideposts requiring action.

Despite their antiquity, you're likely to find elements of these stories to be hauntingly resonant, as well. Again, this is to be expected. For while we like to think that the technological, social, and yes, even metaphysical advancements of our age place us on a plane above our more primitive patriarchs, at the end of the day we are still fundamentally human, and so we are fundamentally susceptible to the same moral and ethical dilemmas that faced those who lived, loved, and died over a millennium ago.

But enough talk from me. I hope you enjoy exploring these stories and their lessons half as much as I enjoyed assembling them for your consideration. Happy reading!

Talese Thumbwick
Senior Professor, Interstellar Ethics
Southwest Protectorate School
17 August/Year 421/S.N.A.

108 Fables for Children

Fable I: The Mighty Kingdom

There was once a kingdom that brought quietude and civility to its people. And security, too. It was a brutal empire, one that defended its ideals without mercy. Its resources were vast, and its wealth was beyond all tell. At the very thought of their emperor, the subjects of this realm trembled- so absolute was his power. The emperor understood that to keep his power- and to grow it, too- he must have an army so large that it would never run out of soldiers, no matter how many were killed. And so the emperor built his great army, and by it he came to rule the world.

Moral: There is strength in numbers.

Fable II: The Wolf, the Badger, and the Bear

A wolf, a badger, and a bear were once best of friends. They lived in the same neighborhood, drank at the same pub, and gathered their families together on the weekends. Their wives, pups, and cubs were best friends, too. One beautiful evening the three friends found themselves sitting around a campfire, under the canopy of an orange and purple sunset, on the banks of a river they had just fished together that day. "Ah...," said the wolf, stretching himself luxuriantly next to the fire, "...the only thing that would make this better is a fresh kill."

"Yeah, a big one, like an elk- something we could all gorge on," agreed the badger enthusiastically. No sooner were those words spoken, then a massive bull elk walked across the far edge of their camp. The three friends were in awe, but true to their predators' instincts, they immediately pounced on the animal, and between them brought it down.

As the wolf and the badger prepared to set themselves on the feast before them, they were met instead by the bear's slashing claws. The bear made quick work of them both. As the eviscerated wolf and badger lay dying atop hot piles of their own pink entrails, the bear drug the elk off a ways and ate it. After all, he's a bear.

Moral: Might makes right.

Fable III: The Owls & the Turkey

There was once a confederacy of learned and well-esteemed owls, renowned for their access to massive amounts of data. They were experts on nearly everything and spoke with conviction on a wide range of topics and theories. They were passionate. They were intense.

One day this group of scholars was congregated under a willow tree next to a pond. They were discussing the best way to prepare a turkey for dinner. "My research shows that frying the bird is the best way to keep it moist," said one owl. "I have it on top authority that roasting is better than frying," said another owl. A heated discussion ensued amongst the group, as each owl had its own informed opinion on how best to cook a turkey. Some said grill, some said smoke, some said brine, some said dry rub; theories spanned the gamut.

As the conversation was reaching its fever pitch, a wild turkey wandered by and overheard the group's discussion. "Excuse me, Ladies and Gentlemen," said the turkey, "but I couldn't help overhearing your debate. Might I suggest that you don't eat turkeys at all, but rather content yourselves with chicken- which I hear is delicious." At this, the owls looked up, then without a word attacked en masse, and using their blade-sharp beaks and talons, they tore the hapless turkey to shreds. Because while it's fine and good to debate on the various methods of cooking a turkey, whether or not one should eat a turkey in the first place is simply not a topic that is up for discussion.
Moral: You may think anything you want, so long as you think like us.

Fable IV: The Dog & the Shadow

There was once a dog who liked to walk on his hind legs when no one was watching. He'd put on trousers, spats, and a porkpie hat and teeter around- happy as a lark- pretending to be a foppish gentleman. Unfortunately for this dog, upright walking was strictly prohibited by town ordinance, so he could only do it in the privacy of his own home, behind closed doors.

One evening the dog was at home, curtains closed, walking around upright. He was really enjoying himself, too- he liked the view from up there. As he was moving about the house taking it all in and feeling quite dandy, the door burst in and four German shepherds in riot gear stormed his apartment and beat the dog unconscious with batons. Authorities were operating off a tip from an unnamed source.
Moral: Anonymity is a sacred right.

Fable V: The Bobcat & the Bunny

A bobcat was crossing a dry arroyo one sunny day when he heard a gentle and guileless voice call to him from the shade of a nearby mesquite tree. It was a fuzzy little bunny, fanning himself with a straw sombrero and smiling ear-to-ear. "Hello, Friend," said the bunny amiably, "...what a fine day to be out for a walk, eh? My name is Bartholomew Bunny; it's a great pleasure to meet you." The bobcat, startled by the bunny's sudden appearance, remained silent. The bunny continued, "I've just been to market and now I'm heading back home with the gold I received from selling my wares. I own the carrot ranch, out past the saguaro forest- maybe you know it?" The bobcat grunted noncommittally. "Well anyhow, it was a propitious day and I sold all I brought with me. It'll be a good winter for my family," the bunny said happily. Silence from the bobcat. "Yes...well...anyhow, my wife and kids will be anxious to see me, so I'd best be getting along." Silence. "You seem like a good sort, Mr. Bobcat. If you ever make it over by our carrot farm, we'd be pleased to put you up as a most-welcome guest. Come by anytime. Well, nice to meet you." Then by way of a handshake, the bunny offered the bobcat his small, fuzzy paw and a heartfelt smile. The bobcat stared at the bunny for half a tick, then ripped his throat out. Then he took the bunny's gold, donned the bunny's sombrero, and made his way out to the carrot ranch- where he fed on the bunny's wife and children, leaving none alive.

Moral: Innocence is for suckers.

Fable VI: The Monkey King

A revered monkey king sat in judgment over a dispute between two of his monkey subjects. The first monkey was quite distraught, because the banana tree behind her house had been picked clean, and she had no bananas now to eat with her toast. "And also," said the angry monkey, "I worked really hard planting and feeding and tending that banana tree, and now I have no bananas. It's not fair!" The monkey king nodded empathetically at the first monkey's words, then spoke, "And what makes you think this monkey (pointing to the second monkey) took your bananas?" he asked. "Oh, I know he didn't take my bananas; he was on a motorcycle trip at the time with my husband George. They're friends, you see. But I did see him shimmy up my tree and take a coconut last season," the first monkey replied, "and nothing ever happened about that."

At this, the monkey king glared accusingly at the second monkey, who sat sheepishly twisting his tail and averting his eyes for shame. "And what do you have to say for yourself?" the monkey king bellowed. "As the lady said, Your Highness, I wasn't even around at the time. I'm clearly innocent of this crime," the second monkey implored. "Not the bananas, you fool- the coconut," said the monkey king sternly. "Oh that... yes," stammered the second monkey. "Well you see, Your Majesty, I really thought all this was going to be about taking the bananas today- and I'm innocent of that!"

"I've heard quite enough," said the monkey king. "I find you guilty of the crime of banana stealing. Thirty days, hard labor. Dismissed!" And all those in the court applauded the monkey king's wisdom, for everyone knows, you can't run a civil society without accountability.
Moral: Vengeance is the highest form of justice.

Fable VII: The Duck's Share

Moods in the barn were at a dangerously high simmer. It seemed each animal was jealous of the next: the cow envied the chicken for its eggs, the chicken envied the pig for its leisure, the pig envied the horse for its strength, and the horse envied the cow for its milk. The only animal that none seemed to envy was the duck. After all, what good is a duck?- at least so thought the other barnyard dwellers. This attitude toward his kind was not lost on the duck, who was rendered equal parts angry and hurt by his neighbors' opinion. "Someday they'll see what a duck is worth," said the duck menacingly to himself, then sat in wait.

Things didn't improve any around the farm- in fact, they worsened. One day shoving broke out between the chicken and the horse, and before long a farmwide punch-up had ensued. As the fur and feathers flew, the duck quietly skirted the violence and snuck into the feed shed. There he found a barrel holding all the farm's honeyed oats- the sweet feed Farmer Dan gave to the animals as a treat when they were well-behaved. While everyone else was fighting, the duck rolled the barrel of oats into the nearby forest and hid it in a briar, for himself. Then he tossed a lit match into the barn's hayloft, and watched with delight as the whole place burned.
Moral: Whatever else may happen, make sure you get yours.

Fable VIII: The Platypus & the Porcupine

There was once a platypus who lived on the banks of a muddy red river. There was nothing he loved more than swimming up and down that river, collecting freshwater shrimp, and BBQing them for his buddies. One day at just such a party, the platypus's friend, the porcupine, made a joke to all their other friends about the small size of the shrimp they were eating. It was a funny joke, because the shrimp were large and delicious, and everyone had a good chuckle at the porcupine's farce. Everyone but the platypus. The platypus was deeply offended by the joke- it made him feel unappreciated for his hard work and hospitality. And though he didn't let on, the platypus never forgot the affront, nor ever fully forgave the porcupine.

Many years passed; the platypus continued to grill shrimp and throw parties for his friends, the porcupine continued to attend- all the while unaware of his host's ire. And then it happened: one day the porcupine made another lighthearted quip to the crowd about the weather, and that was all the platypus needed to hear. He snuck up behind the porcupine, drew a poison dagger from his boot, and slid the blade into the porcupine's spleen- all the way to the hilt, just like a toothpick through a cocktail wiener. Then the platypus kicked the dead porcupine into the river- where he floated face-down toward the rocky falls that roared in wait, just around the bend.

Moral: Never give offense to anyone about anything ever.

Fable IX: The Clever Dove

There was once a beautiful white-winged dove that lived at the top of a cottonwood tree, deep in the high desert. All the animals of this place respected the dove because she was a creature of peace and wisdom, and always had a word of kindness for any soul that happened across her path.

One day, a peregrine falcon alighted on an arm of the cottonwood tree where the dove lived, seeking rest from his long flight. The dove fluttered down from her top branch to greet the falcon and offer him provisions. He was a taciturn bird, and the dove could immediately see in the falcon's eyes the malice that was in his heart. Giving nothing away, the dove

"Where did you find that thing?"

"Huh?" I said, looking up from my story. Simon was standing above me. "Where did you find that thing?" he repeated. "Oh, on that shelf- next to your plasma frame," I answered, pointing. "Yeah, that's not mine- not sure how it got there. It belongs to Estrella; it was her great-grandfather's or something. Just throw it over there," he said dismissively. So I did.

"Thirsty? How about some water?" he asked next. "Yep, sounds great, thanks." Then we headed to the de-sal spigot for a quick splash, and got back to it. There was lots left to do, and the day was only getting hotter.

****

IQ600

Once upon a time, not so far from where you sit now, the smartest being in the history of the world came onto this planet. His name was Isaiah Jackson, and he was unlike anything humanity had ever seen- or will ever see again.

By the age of 2, Isaiah Jackson spoke nine languages. By the age of 5 he had created a working model for cold fusion. By the age of 10, he had solved the mysteries of quantum gravity and antimatter. At the age of 16, he introduced the world to "logical operatic cubism," a theory of his own devise, considered to have had a greater impact on art, music, and philosophy than the ideas of the Chinese & Greeks, combined.

Isaiah Jackson's genius was so profound and his impact on humanity was so great, that it was openly debated by the pundits of the day whether he was an angel or an alien. It was widely assumed he was one or the other. Nearly everyone took for granted that he was not human-born.

By the time he was 35 years old, Isaiah Jackson had transformed the fields of medicine, transportation, environmentalism, education, architecture, law, and economics- and many more besides. Without question, the world with Isaiah Jackson in it was a place of unprecedented intellectual enlightenment. And yet, Isaiah Jackson still had work to do.

It came to pass one day that Isaiah Jackson was surveying the world he'd created and was reflecting on the advancements he had begotten, when a great sadness fell upon him. He realized that despite all that he had done for the betterment of Mankind, still men sought dominion and control over one another. Despite improvements to virtually every category of living, the human urge to kill and subjugate persisted. Isaiah

Jackson realized that war was the one human affliction he hadn't yet cured; and he knew it was the only one that mattered. So next, with these thoughts in mind, Isaiah Jackson decided to disappear.

He dropped away from everything and everyone and he went into hiding, so that he could meditate on notions of peace- and devise a way that Earth might have it. And Isaiah Jackson was gone for a very long time. So long in fact, that many believed he had died in seclusion. And though the world mourned the loss of its greatest mind, life went on. Humanity continued to benefit from Isaiah Jackson's genius, and people everywhere continued to maim their kind.

Then one day- to the surprise and delight of all- Isaiah Jackson returned. And the people of Earth exalted and they said to him, "Tell us, Isaiah Jackson, where did you go and what have you learned? And what will you give us next?" And Isaiah Jackson answered them thusly:

"I am not staying long, Friends, for I have found great solace in the wilderness- away from Mankind and its violence- and I seek to return there soon. Besides, there's nothing left for me to give you- my best ideas are already yours. But I will share one last secret I have discovered before I go. It's the greatest secret of all, because it is the key to human harmony. Do but this one thing and you shall live forever after without war, and Humanity will finally know peace."

"What is it?! What is it?!" the people asked excitedly, for they felt themselves on the threshold of Isaiah Jackson's greatest teaching. "Tell us!" the people begged, "tell us and we will do it. You have never steered us wrong, and we believe everything you say, because your mind is the master of our race. We trust you wholeheartedly, Isaiah Jackson. What must we do?"

"The thing you must do is this," Isaiah Jackson answered them gently, "you must be kind to each other. If you see someone who needs something you have, share with them freely and seek nothing in return. If you see a way to lighten another's burden, do this thing for them. If you have no need of a thing another has, do not seek it from them; for 'want' is not the same as 'need.' And teach your children to teach their children this lesson, too. For when every last person of this place does this, your world will finally know peace."

“Yes!” cried the people, “the final piece; the thing that will finally make everything perfect! We will do it! We will do it, Isaiah Jackson- thank you for this wisdom!”

“Remember,” Isaiah Jackson said solemnly, “every single man, woman, and child must do this thing, or peace will elude you; and then every single man, woman, and child will despair. That’s all I have for you. Now I must go. Goodbye.”

And as the world rejoiced in anticipation of the peace that was sure to visit them, Isaiah Jackson slipped quietly away.

****

she is a drug to me

"You are a drug to me," I said.
"That's not a compliment," she said.
"I meant it as a compliment," I said.
"I'm even writing a story about it. It's called, 'she is a drug to me.' Actually, that's only exactly as far as I've gotten on it so far. That and maybe one line- I can't remember. But the title is true, so I'm sure it will go somewhere," I said.
"Drugs are bad for you. They ruin your life. I'm afraid it's not a compliment," she smiled.
"Yes," I smiled back, reaching for her, "I see your point."

****

youth sleuth and the mystery of the unknown thing (abridged)

Youth Sleuth and the Mystery of the Unknown Thing

CHAPTER I
A Dangerous Situation

"Gee whiz, Tucker," George exclaimed enthusiastically, "this sure beats chasing bad guys through back alleys, don't it?" "You said it, Georgie," replied Tucker McDrew lazily. The two boys reclined on lounge chairs in the late morning sun. George was eating a ham sandwich, Tucker had his eyes closed and was sinking into the golden mellow of his morning meds.

Child detective and local teen celebrity, Tucker McDrew, was taking a much-needed break from sleuthing to relax and recuperate after solving his latest caper, *"The Mystery of the Headless Torso."* What a doozy that one had been- Tucker had barely escaped with his life! At one point the boy sherlock was abducted to a log cabin along a secluded stretch of Dixon Lake. Thank goodness Tucker's best friend and sleuthing sidekick- George Beschet- had been there to save him from those murderous thugs before they roughed him up too much worse. George often saved Tucker's bacon when the young detective involved himself in things best left to the police.

Though Tucker never accepted compensation for solving his many cases- Truth and Justice were Tucker McDrew's wage- he wasn't above accepting a favor from time to time. In fact, it was a favor that had landed the two boys where they were now. So pleased had Colonel Stonenut been at having received back his stolen spyglass after the torso affair, that he treated Tucker and George to a week of repair at the Glenview Heights Hospitality Retreat and Salutarium. The boys were recouping in the estate's fresh mountain air- taking in sun on the east wing portico.

George, a fat but friendly seventeen year old, had an unhealthy relationship with food and compensated by being extra enthusiastic and outgoing. Adults were constantly praising his "great attitude." Surprisingly, though George was fat he wasn't stupid; in fact he wasn't even lazy. George kept a vigilant- nearly pathological- watch over his friend Tucker at all times, and was constantly on the lookout for villains and clues. George looked up from his sandwich now, as something caught his eye. "Hold on then, what's this?" said the husky boy, wiping his mouth on his sleeve.

A porter wearing a red pillbox hat, brass-buttoned tunic, and white gloves approached the boys and wordlessly extended a sterling tray toward Tucker. Upon the tray sat a fresh sprig of sweetpea blossom. Next to the purple bloom sat a telegram. Tucker took the communiqué without comment or eye contact then waved the messenger off. With a quick nod and sharp click of heels, the porter briskly about-faced and departed.

Tucker's father, Stewart McDrew, was a well-known attorney, private detective, and workaholic. An accomplished sleuth in his own right, Mr. McDrew was best known for having brought down the Crimini Crime Family in the caper the local paper dubbed, *"The Case of the Angry Mob."* Mr. McDrew was a handsome devil; he slayed it with the ladies. Tucker- an only child- was often left alone for long stretches of time while his father worked and chased. Communication between the two happened primarily via telegram- similar to the one just delivered. Mrs. McDrew skipped town years previous, and lived upstate with her longtime boyfriend, Ned.

"One guess who this is from!" Tucker said smilingly, then he opened the note and read with boyish enthusiasm. As Tucker studied the telegram, a confused expression darkened the teen's attractive features. He wrinkled his brow and thought for a moment, his detective's curiosity on full display. "Well hopping heck and hambones, don't keep a fella hanging- what's the note say, Tuck?" asked George anxiously. "I don't think this is from my dad, George," Tucker answered his friend in confusion. "It says, 'get down.' Get down from whe...?"

At that moment, a deafening roar filled the air. An explosion! And in the salutarium, no less! Blunt chunks of wreckage sprayed everywhere- like a thousand cannonballs being fired simultaneously across everything, taking out everything. All was carnage. Wet meat and gore strewed across the manicured sloping lawn, and crying moans were the only sounds heard in the bomb's numbing wake. Even those away from the blast suffered- many patients rolled on the ground in agony, blood pouring from their ruptured ears.

Amidst this chaos, a shape emerged from beneath a pile of dusty ruin. It was Tucker McDrew, and he was miraculously unhurt! The heroic teen gumshoe beat a cloud of dirt from his chest, coughed twice, then in a chalky voice yelled for his missing friend: "George! Where are you?" An arm pushed feebly up through the debris. "George!" Tucker yelled again, then scrambled to free his friend from underneath the pile of rubble.

George rose from the wreckage dusty and bloodied; his face on one side was badly damaged. Glass in many sharp shapes and sizes protruded from it. "George- your face!" exclaimed Tucker in alarm. "Oh I'll be fine," said George matter-of-factly, as the blood poured down his chubby cheeks. "It didn't hit nothing worth mentioning... But at least one thing *is* worth mentioning for sure," he continued with a good-natured chuckle. "What's that?" asked Tucker McDrew. "Next time there's a note saying 'get down,'" George grinned winkingly, "let's make sure we get down faster!"

****

CHAPTER VIII
A Curious Stranger

Tucker and George were on the beach hurriedly repacking their chutes, working frantically to store their jump gear before the hurricane rising about them gained any more strength. "Wowzer gee-willikers, Tuck," yelled George over the shrieking wind, "looks like we hit the LZ just in time!" "You can say that again, George!" Tucker yelled back, as he squinted and dodged against the sand-swirling debris. "We'd better get out of here, and fast!" Tucker continued, "Let's go find that warehouse- it can't be far." Then the boys grabbed their kit and raced up the beach toward the evacuated town of Brackish Bay. A raging purple sky howled down upon them.

For nearly a week now, the residents of Brackish Bay had been rushing to get their homes boarded and sandbagged ahead of Hurricane Nancy- the apocalyptic superstorm that was fixing to hit their town square on the jaw. What's more, over the last couple days before the storm's arrival, federal disaster agents and local authorities had been hustling everyone out of town in accordance with the Governor's evacuation order. Tucker, true to rapscallion form, had decided to ignore the fiat and instead chase a clue straight into the heart of the tempest. As a result, the young investigators now found themselves walking the empty streets of a buttressed and deserted place. Big fat George pulled a candy bar out of his canvas knapsack and started munching; he was a stress eater.

"Jeepers, Tucker, looks like we're the only ones in this entire town!" George exclaimed nervously between bites. "I think you might be right, Georgie," Tucker replied. "I wonder if that means Mr. Masterson is gone, too?" George quizzed. He had finished his first candy bar and was opening a second; his knapsack was full of them. "Only one way to be sure," Tucker responded, "find the warehouse and we'll find the clue. Hello, I think that's it there now!"

As the boys rounded a corner, the brick facade of a massive warehouse greeted them. A single door was the only disruption to the building's north facing front. Across the door was a red stenciled sign reading: *Larkspur Ship & Receive Co.* "This is it!" enthused George enthusiastically. "Let's go find that clue!" The boys tried the handle on the building's steel-reinforced door, but it was locked. Moving around to the building's east side, the teen sleuths found the window to a small ground floor office. Using a nearby rock, Tucker smashed the glass pane and the boys scrambled through the jagged hole into the darkened space. Over the years, Tucker had climbed through many windows of his own breaking; he was quite agile and good at avoiding injury. Unexpectedly, so was George; tubby teen that he was.

Once inside, the young detectives clicked on their flashlights and swung them in a wide arc around the room, taking quick inventory of their spartan surroundings. A nearly-bare office revealed itself to the light's sweeping beams. After searching through the office's dented steel desk, the youths searched through the office's dented steel filing cabinet- but found no clue. Passing from the office, Tucker and George entered next onto the warehouse's massive main floor and into its breathtaking expanse of darkness and void.

Security lights demarcating the area's broad walkways were pinpricks of luminosity against the cavernous black of the warehouse. Rather than diminish, these feeble glows served only to accentuate the Stygian maw that swallowed everything all and around. Rows upon rows of steel-braced industrial shelving- stacked it seemed with every last box- reeled off in both directions and ascended toward the unseeable ceiling; every aspect fading to vantablack. "This place is big," said Tucker lamely, as he gawked into the enormous nothing. "We'd better split up. I'll go left, you go right. If you find a clue, George, blow your whistle."

"Right-O!" spunked George, then off he bounded into the direction Tucker had commanded, meager light from his electric hand torch leading the way.

While George disappeared down and around some invisible corner, Tucker McDrew took up his own light and made his way down the nearest long row of shelves. As he walked the endless aisles, Tucker shone his light from time to time on random boxes, reading their labels and hoping against hope to stumble onto some hint of what Mr. Masterson was up to. "The clue has got to be here somewhere," Tucker spoke aloud to no one, his small voice punctuating the near-silence of the place. Faintly in the faraway distance, Nancy could be heard screaming her destruction.

As Tucker McDrew wandered the warehouse haystack searching for his needle, a rubber-soled figure emerged silently from the shadows and began to follow the teen hero at a small distance. The menacing figure was black clad, and masked his face with an also-black balaclava. He carried a heavy steel wrench in his meaty grip. Unaware of the danger, Tucker continued to search randomly but intensely for any indication that might move his case forward, as the malefic figure quietly closed the space between them. So engrossed was he in his hunt that Tucker didn't hear the creeping man nor sense his ill-intent as the wrench was quietly raised then swung down violently, striking the unaware Tucker right between the shoulder blades. Tucker was knocked down hard by the hit and lay in a limp lump- dazed and confused- as the shadowy assailant stood above his prey and raised the wrench once more, winding up to deliver Tucker McDrew a finishing death blow.

The killer's weapon reached its apex and was just beginning its downward swing, when from seemingly nowhere a rocket shot hit the attacker from behind, sending the wrench flying and flinging him over Tucker's moveless body into the steel racks beyond. It was George(!) crashing in from the shadows to deliver a perfect form tackle to the small of the attacker's back! Hurtling himself- like a chubby teen comet- into harm's way, so as to save his friend Tucker from certain doom!

A savage fight for control of the fallen wrench ensued between George and the man. While the masked assailant was the bigger, stronger, and quicker of the two, George had the heart of a lion and the fight of ten honey badgers in him. The combatants wrestled, clawed, bit, and punched at each other, all the while tussling for the wrench- that skittered and spun away and around the two fighters most frustratingly. What seemed hours was but a few tense moments of violent scrambling, when against the odds George's blind fingers pawed across the wrench and gripped it. He swung the thing wild and hard, and with a wet melon sound met his weapon squarely upon his adversary's skull. The man went out like a light and lay still as a stone, but for his right foot that quivered faintly.

George lay next to his unmoving opponent, heaving for air in the wake of battle- completely spent from the fight's effort. After a few moments of hyperventilating, he rolled to his side and retched violently, spewing a puddle of half-digested candy, then slumped next to it and gasped- too tired to move. Tucker by now had risen shakily, and walked slowly over to recovering George- whom he knelt beside, then helped to his feet after a few minutes of recuperation. "Guess we'd better look under this guy's kimono," Tucker said, nodding toward the body. Then he reached down, gripped the goo sticky mask, and pulled.

Like a jack 'o lantern abandoned to the mid-November sun, the stranger's skull was sunken in on itself; a wide dent across his temple revealing the spot where George's wrench had found its mark. The man's eyes were open, but unseeing. Neither boy recognized him. "Well I guess this fella's days of wrench clunking are over," said George sunnily, having by now recovered his breath and his mood. He kicked playfully at the dead man's twitching boot. "I'll check his pockets, maybe he has some identification," Tucker replied, as he reached into the corpse's trousers and rifled about. After a few moments of searching, Tucker's hand froze in place and a wide smile augmented his handsome mien. Slowly, he withdrew a dull-glowing object from the body's right front pants pocket. Tucker McDrew held the pulsating figurine toward his friend and said excitedly, "Well what do you know, George Old Chap; it looks like we just found the clue!"

****

CHAPTER XIII
A Mysterious Memento

While Tucker McDrew struggled against his restraints aboard the submarine, above the lake George was on a stakeout- wholly unaware of his friend's danger below. Per Tucker's instruction, George had been tailing the blond man's blue convertible all morning, logging his whereabouts and keeping on the lookout for any sign of the missing girl. George had followed the man to a petrol station, where an attendant was topping off the car's tank and cleaning its windscreen now. As his car was being serviced, the driver crossed the street to make a call from a nearby phone booth. "What's this guy up to?" George asked himself inwardly. He was eating a cake while he spied. An entire cake. All to himself, no utensils. It seemed George was spiraling down a vortex of intense self-loathing.

After finishing his call, the towheaded man recrossed the street, tipped the station attendant, and put back to the road- heading south on Salisbury Street. George set down the snack, then used his slacks as a napkin and pulled his jalopy into traffic- following behind the convertible at a safe distance. The two drivers made their way across the train tracks and into the neighborhood of Bayport Green: the godforsaken, killing part of town. Despite the thousands of calories George had been mindlessly consuming all morning, his stomach still growled angrily.

The two cars wove and wandered their way through the potholed streets, passing a menagerie of lost souls and orphaned shopping carts along the way. George was able to keep an undetectable distance from his mark, as the man's blond hair and convertible made him easy to spot. After some time, the blue car pulled into the trash-strewn parking lot of The Sugar Shack, a greasy club for "gentlemen" wedged between a liquor store and a pawn shop. The man alighted from his vehicle and entered the place, unaware of the watching eyes of his tubby teenage tail.

"I can't go in there," thought George to himself, "I'm too young. Plus, nice boys don't look at naked ladies." George wasn't really that into girls, and girls were decidedly not that into George. After sitting in the car for a few moments stressing over his options, George decided to search the blond man's convertible for clues. "I'll have to be quick. And sly," George thought to himself. He left his car at the pawn shop, then slunk next door and over to the blond man's vehicle. His attempt to look inconspicuous was completely unnecessary; this was the kind of neighborhood where you always only mind your own business.

George looked into the car's backseat, but it was empty. The front seat was clean too, but for an ashtray stuffed with cigarette butts and a collection of crumpled food wrappers in the passenger footwell. "Mmm, burgers..." George noted subconsciously, as he made his way into the glove compartment and searched its contents. He combed past a rusty jackknife, a tire gauge, and a poorly folded Wirt County streets map before discovering the vehicle's registration coupon. "Good night, Joe!" George declared aloud, "This car belongs to Mr. Masterson! Now that's what I call a nifty clue. I have to go find Tucker and let him know!" At that moment, a heavy hand fell thickly across George's shoulder and spun him with unfriendly force. "I told you I'd find you again, punk," a familiar voice sneered. George's stomach dropped: he was looking directly into the bloodshot eyes of the red haired man!

Without hesitation, George smashed the crown of his skull onto the bridge of his enemy's nose, smearing the meat of it over toward the murderer's right cheek. Blood gushed, but the man didn't budge and his eyes never blinked. George's heart went cold with the knowledge of what he was up against. In a rapid burst of three thrusts, the red haired man shanked George in the stomach with a snub nosed screwdriver he held in his right hand. The wounds weren't mortal, but they were deep enough. Blood began to ooze around and over George's belly, soaking the front of his cake-stained trousers. At the moment George registered his stabbing, he thrust his knee up and into his attacker's groin, as hard as he could; a direct hit. The red haired man dropped his weapon, fell to the ground, and writhed about in an agonized ball.

George took advantage of his window and hobble-sprinted away from the red haired man and back toward his car- the throbbing pain in his stomach overridden by adrenaline. George fumbled briefly with his keys, then opened the door and jumped in. He started and revved the engine, then threw his transmission to reverse, and then to forward gear. With a brief fish-tail and spit of gravel, George raced out of the parking lot and nosed north, back toward Glenview Heights. As he drove off, George looked at his wristwatch and thought, "I've got to get to the rendezvous point, Tucker will be waiting for me. I sure hope he got good news at the dock." His wounds were ignored.

George drove exactly the posted speed limit and obeyed all traffic rules on his way back to town. "Don't get stopped doing something dumb, like speeding. Come on now, George- you gotta think like Tucker," the badly injured boy thought to himself as he drove. He was headed toward the boys' sleuthing headquarters and their regular place of rendezvous: Tucker McDrew's dad's house.

As he rounded the McDrew's quarter-mile driveway, arriving upon their glass and steel bachelor pad, George's mind was racing. He was eager to tell Tucker about the connection he'd discovered between the blond haired man and Mr. Masterson; not to mention his re-encounter with the red haired man. Questions kept jumbling through his mind: 'What was the connection between the convertible and the man at the dock? If the blond haired man really was looking for the missing girl, what was he doing at The Sugar Shack? And how does the red haired man keep finding me?' George was anxious to sort through these mysteries with Tucker McDrew. But where was he?

Tucker usually parked his lifted truck in the shade of the carport, but there was no sign of it now. "Hmm," George mused, "Tucker should have beat me here by at least an hour- I hope he's ok. Guess I'll wait for him inside." Then he parked his beater near the fountain and limped his way through the home's minimalist entry garden. George arrived at the front door and made to ring the bell, alerting the housekeeper to his presence, when his toe nudged against an object on the front mat. "How now- what's this?" said George to himself, as he bent over with some effort and picked up a small box. There was an envelope taped to its top. It was addressed to 'Mr. George Beschet.' George opened the envelope and slid out a lined index card. Written in pencil with a hasty hand, the card read: *Tucker McDrew says "hi."* Intuition went off in George's mind like a hand grenade and his blood seemed for just a moment to stop pumping. With a dread-filled heart, George put aside the note and moved to open the box. He lifted its lid trepidatiously, and a horrified gasp escaped him. George had to look twice to be sure, and even still he had to ask (though really he already knew): "Is that... is that a *human ear*?!"

****

CHAPTER XX
The Next Episode

"Secret Service! Hands up!" yelled the brawny man. He wore tactical body armor and pointed a machine gun at the surprised jewel thieves. The red dot of his laser sight bore unwaveringly into the chest of Headmaster Strop. Similar dots adorned the chests of the other three gangsters, too. The Secret Service agent and six members of his team had quietly approached the group from the east, and had the criminals pinned just outside the tunnel now. Johnson moved to take aim at the agent, but before he could raise his pistol even above his waist, he was shot through the head by a sniper- the team's eighth and hidden member. Upon seeing their fellow goon's fate, Hernadez and Valetti quickly dropped their weapons, raised their hands, and went quietly into custody. Headmaster Strop was not so docile, however, and struggled mightily against the authorities' iron grip.

"Curse you, Tucker McDrew!" the headmaster spat with rage. "You've foiled my plans for the last time, you meddling snoop! I'll kill you! Do you hear me? I'll kill you!" Strop went screaming and kicking all the way to the squad car- into which he was unceremoniously dumped. Then Headmaster Strop and his murderous fury were driven away, to be booked downtown at the Third Street Station. Strop could be seen silently hollering and gesticulating against the car's window as it made its way down the road and around the corner. "Jeez 'o Pete," said Field Agent Kade, "what's got him so riled up?" Kade had come onto the scene just behind the tactical unit and was untying Tucker and George now. "Shucks, he's just sore 'cuz Tucker outwitted him twice," chuckled George as he rubbed the circulation back into his sausagey wrists. "First Tucker got the headmaster to spill his guts on the submarine- on just about everything you can imagine! Tucker got Strop to give up details on the heist, the sabotage- even their escape plan. And then- just now- Strop told us all about his double-cross on Mr. Masterson; and even where to find the missing girl, too!" George added admiringly. "And it's all right here on tape," Tucker said, patting his chest pocket with a smile. "The good citizens of Glenview Heights owe you a great debt of gratitude, Tucker McDrew," Field Agent Kade lauded, manfully slapping the teen superstar on his perfect shoulder. George silently smiled broadly next to his famous friend.

At that moment, a seriously handsome man in a perfectly cut suit rushed breathlessly into view. He was trailed closely by three uniformed police officers- all with weapons drawn. Upon seeing the special agents milling about the crime scene, the seriously handsome man and his police companions slowed to a walk and re-holstered their weapons. The seriously handsome man charmed jokingly as he approached the group smilingly- saying, "Ahoy, Lads! Looks like we just missed the excitement! Hopefully, you left a bad guy or two for us!" "Dad!" cried Tucker, and ran to the seriously handsome man. The boy and his father embraced. "I came as soon as I got your telegram, Son," Stewart McDrew said sternly but with tender eyes. "I know you did, Dad- thanks for being here. I can always count on you when the chips are down," Tucker effused. His father beamed. Tucker enjoyed the moment and ignored the fact that it had been 2 days since he'd sent the SOS.

"Hot bacon and flapjacks," George playfully exasperated, "that was one wild case! If we needed a rest before last week, we *really* need a rest now!" "You said it, Georgie," Tucker replied gleefully, "I don't imagine we'll ever get another case as exciting as that one." But Tucker McDrew was mistaken. Unbeknownst to the boys, they would soon find themselves embroiled in a case even more dangerous and exciting, when the young detectives stumble onto *The Disappearing Mystery of the Invisible Stone*.

"Now that we've solved the case, I guess there's only one thing left to do," Smiling George smiled smilingly. "What's that?" asked Tucker McDrew. "Let's EAT!!!" George screamed maniacally, his voice cracking with emotion and his eyes welling with tears. Then everyone had a good laugh at George.

He was a hungry boy with pudgy fingers.

****

three dollar mule

Now I wouldn't trade my Sweet Rebecca for the moon, but sometimes I swear that woman drives me like a three dollar mule. I recognize it's fair and right for a woman to need her man to do her bidding from time to time, and I'm happy to do it almost all the time. Truth is, most often you'd be hard-pressed to find me passing up a chance to put my girl first. But let me tell you, Friend, there's times when I just gotta get a hot minute to myself. I'm sure any guy out there with a gal will agree, a little space is a thing we men sometimes need.

As it was, I was having a day just like that, just the other day: one where it serves the communal interests that I should get out of the house for a spell- lest I do or say something I wish I hadn't. So I stopped myself mid-sentence, put down the heavy object, held a deep breath and let it out real slow. Just like Doc Trygg showed me. Then I gave my Becca a peck on the cheek and told her I'd be back in not too long, and in any case not later than supper. Didn't really matter where I was going- least not to me- I just needed a change of location and maybe some alternate company.

I got in the van and drove for a bit, putting my mind on autopilot and letting the tide drift me where it would. After a while, I kinda blinked myself outta my daydream and gauged my place in time. I had gone where I always go when left to my own devices: straight down to the water. I was maybe two, three blocks off the drydocks, when an idea took root, and a darn good one, too.

I headed down and over to Mission Boulevard and found a spot for the van right out in front of Uncle Louie's. Providence, it seemed, was smiling on my designs. Uncle Louie's is the local public house and the primary source of relief from the various thirsts, appetites, and miseries that afflict the Puerto Flamingo blue collars: we stevedores, longshoremen, and sailors who people this salty clapboard hamlet. I don't know how long the place has been here, but by the looks of it I'd say about forever.

It's not much to see from the outside. Originally, it was probably a warehouse or service depot for the now defunct Vancouver-to-La Paz rail line- whose overgrown tracks and busted up ties cross through the weedy lot, just behind the bar's rotting brick building. A rust choked and also rotting tin roof serves to (sort of) keep the rain off those within. Teetering on the warped sidewalk out in front of the place is a beaten up A-frame chalkboard- the bar's only signage. Written in smeared cursive with white chalk up against a green background, both sides of the board read the same: Louie's. Beneath the word, on one side of the sign someone has taken a swipe at drawing a spiny lobster- this time in red chalk. So apparently displeased was the artist with this cross-eyed and wonk-kneed rendering, they didn't even bother with an illustration on the sign's other side.

Though it would be tough to find any building exterior- short of a haunted slaughterhouse- with less curb appeal, the interior of Uncle Louie's is surprisingly not as stabby as you'd think, and a whole lot more inviting, too. As expected, the lights burn mellow and low. As expected, there's something scattered across the time-beaten pine floor; sawdust or peanut shells or hay or something. As expected, there are faded, greasy black & whites hanging akimbo at haphazard intervals all around the place- big caught fish in some, intrepid ships' crews or storied sea captains in others.

What's unexpected about Uncle Louie's are the sounds of the place. In most of the world's seafaring taverns, you'll find plenty of cursing and hollering and no small amount of fighting- all above the blare of some thumping and thought-blasting musicnoise. In fact the first thing you'd look to hear in a place like this are the brash yowls of brawny men and tawdry women. Not so at Uncle Louie's. The mood here is anything but roughcast. First off, the tenor of Uncle Louie's is informed by the music of the masters that floats gently above the space, infusing its air: Bach, Mozart, Rachmaninov, Beethoven, *et alia*. Uncle Louie maintains an extensive collection of vinyl masterpieces, which he rotates unendingly on the ancient turntable he keeps behind the bar. These sounds have a strange effect on the room- they tend to soften sharp edges, and vivify fraternal sympathies. Whatever the burdens of life one might bring with them into Uncle Louie's, one seldom leaves with the same. There are just too many friendly folks in this place to let you suffer such a heavy load all by yourself. And as for yelling, the only howls you're likely to hear here are those attending laughter and good cheer. By all accounts, Uncle Louie's is a happy place.

It is generally concurred that there are three primary points of interest revealing Uncle Louie's to be a, if not charming, at least idiosyncratic establishment. First are the saloon-style swinging doors that offer entrance to the place but nothing in the way of protection from weather or foe. Uncle Louie has never put anything but swinging doors on the front of his joint. No locks, no gates, no nothing. That's because Uncle Louie's never closes. It's open 24/7/365, and always has been. It's also because Uncle Louie never leaves Uncle Louie's. There's an increasingly-believable urban legend that says Uncle Louie has never once stepped foot away from Uncle Louie's since its opening some 25 or maybe 50 years ago. For what it's worth, in the eighteen years I've been coming here, I've never seen him outside the premises. Not once.

Second point of interest at Uncle Louie's is the life-sized, hi-res, and well-lit photograph of Uncle Louie's buck naked ex-wife, Brenda, that hangs above the bar. All twenty-nine stone of her. The photographer had her lying on her side across a rug or table or some such thing with her elbow propped up and her head in her hand, so the photo's pose and placement give the impression that she's lounging across the top of the bar well, all chutzpah and lady flesh. It's a rather imposing scene and might even be off-putting, if not for the enigmatic charm that emanates from Brenda and her naughty, knowing smirk. If Uncle Louie loves his ex-wife half as much as he loves this photo of his ex-wife, it's a mystery why it didn't work out between them. At least ten times a day, Uncle Louie devises some pretext to rise from his corner stool behind the bar and pass by Brenda's likeness, each time looking up to her smiling down at him and muttering *sotto voce*, "Ah, my beautiful bumblebee..."

Third though never least of the eccentricities awaiting visitors to Uncle Louie's- and the real draw for me to this place- is its patrons, who present- if nothing else- a rather motley view. Anyone who's spent time drinking in a working seaport can attest to this old chestnut: no fisherman's net will ever draw from the deep a creature more rare and strange than that what's to be found in a dockyard pub. And true to form, Uncle Louie's is full of odd fish.

I took up my favorite seat, about halfway down the fifty foot bar, then mimed 'howdy' to Mojo, who finished what he was doing and brought me a drink. As I sipped my Hendrick's and lime, listening my way through the first movement of Vivaldi's *L'inverno*, a deep and familiar voice boomed just behind my right shoulder: "Ah, to pass peaceful, contented days before a roaring hearth- whilst beyond yon door pours down the winter rain..." I didn't need to turn around- but I did- to see standing there the man I knew I would.

Rising six foot five if he's an inch, with the belly of a panda and the laugh of a howler monkey, was fellow barsitter and inveterate scallywag, Milo Olson ('Mr. Milo,' if you please). Wearing surf baggies, flip flops, and a tank top, Mr. Milo had swapped his pierside crane operator's uniform of hardhat and steel toes for this less formal, after-hours ensemble. If there's anything more noticeable than Mr. Milo's girth and elevation, it's just his hair- he has lots of it. In fact, it seems every part of this present-day viking sprouts some amount of curly ginger wool- a premise supported by his exposed legs, arms, shoulders, neck, fingers, toes, and feet, all of which were on display and all of which are jaw-droppingly hirsute. All this in addition to his shoulder-length ponytail and chest-length beard; both of which undoubtedly host domicile to some untold number of furry little critters.

It had been some time since I'd last seen Mr. Milo, and we embraced heartily, as long-separated-pranksters-reunited are wont to do. Truth is, I hadn't even heard he was back. So I asked him, "What's the news, Mr. Milo?" and he tells me he's just finished placating certain camps up north related to, "minor infractions and misunderstandings between former business partners," as he put it. Whatever the previous discords, Mr. Milo seemed confident that these last four months have balanced all books between parties, at least to the satisfaction of the Law. "But if I know you," I said next, "it isn't so much *where* you've been, as *what* you've been doing that commands most interest." Mr. Milo hooted warmly at this patent gospel, then launched himself into the tale of his most recent exploits.

(It's important to note here, Reader: when listening to one of Mr. Milo's recounts, the following breakdown generally holds... roughly 50% of what he says is accurate, about 30% of what he says is well-intentioned fiction, and roughly 10% is an outright lie. The remaining 10% of what Mr. Milo reports is thoroughly unverifiable and should be regarded by the listener with utmost suspicion.)

His tale wound about, around, and through, and covered a fair bit of ground while he told it. He started with his cellmate ("Name a' Dustin Fleck was my bunkie- crypto broker from Rancho Cucamonga. Got in crosswise with his girlfriend's old man; fella who happens to be a private dick and one-time cop. Anyhow, Old Fleck had eight weeks for fighting- though I don't know how, I never met a softer soul. The two of us got along like cousins..."); then wandered by the topic of work furlough ("Kept bumping into this chap named 'Langhorn' or 'Longhorn' or something for a bit too. He got pinched hanging paper outside of Nuevo Viejo, but not so bad that he couldn't go about his weekday job at the tracks. He'd meet up with us on the weekends to grab garbage off the highway. Always had a couple of ponies he'd put on your radar for a Jackson. Nice enough guy. Asthmatic..."); then even got into the food (I was humping boxes one day on KP with a bloke named 'Jersey' - British fella, swift with a head butt- when I noticed from the label we were humping frozen meat. You know what they feed you at County? Grade D: Fit For Human Consumption. You believe that? Just above what you'd feed a dog. Ah well, at least it was better than what we got in the navy...) before veering off into the true wilds of his imagination.

We were coming off some story of his in a fit of laughter. He and I were catching our breath and holding our sides in the way you do when you're telling those sea stories that should never be retold. At the end of this great guffaw, Mr. Milo says to me, still panting, "You know, Tommy... it doesn't do you...no good, to be too good." "Hear, hear," I said, and drank. "No, I mean it, Tom," he says in reply, having now caught his breath, and looking me straight in the eye, his with a mischievous gleam. "Haven't I ever told you the story of *The Very Honest Man*?" "No you have not." "This is one you really need to hear, Tommy. Allow me to regale you." "Yes, please do." That was our exchange. Then Mr. Milo said the following:

So as you know I have the tendency to skip in and outta County on occasion; one might even be tempted to name it a habit. It's not a point I can argue against. But mind you now, Tommy, it's not 'cause I'm so bad, per se, but more because I have a natural propensity for questioning those whom Providence has tapped with the mantle of authority. Unfortunately for me, there's nothing Power hates more than having its logic called to question. So it seems I just can't stay on the side of things those in charge want me to. But that's neither here nor there for now. My point is that I'm no stranger to the accommodations and various recreations offered guests by the well-meaning folks at the Rosarito County Jail.

Truth be told, County's not so bad. Heck, it's not even mostly bad. Sure you're in the clank, and that's no fun, but the thing is, most everyone there is short-timing, so most everyone's in a pretty good mood. That doesn't carry for the hard cases, of course- of which there are plenty some- but the thing with them is, they're all treading water in that Purgatory between verdict and sentence, so their minds are well occupied and not seeking out insult or trouble. The whole thing makes for a pretty kind jam.

Now do you remember a couple years back when I went up for that few weeks over the grass cutting incident with Nuñez? Raw deal, that, but anyhow, I was there and you might recall it. Well I had occasion during that stint to pull gardening duty with a fella named Ricky- French Canadian dude who was hanging around County waiting on a big verdict. He had the saddest eyes of any man I've ever seen. We were pulling weeds in the breeze one day, under a big blue sky and I just couldn't figure out how anyone could be anything less than contented on a day like that. You know I can't stand the company of someone in distress- not if I can do a thing to help ease their strain- so I ask the guy if he might not like to hear a story about a girl I knew from Amarillo- one that's sure to give him a chuckle, and shorten his face, to boot. He doesn't say anything at first- just keeps pulling weeds, head down- then after a couple ticks he looks up at me and says, 'Oh, I guess not. But tell you what, Guy- how about I give you one, instead.' So I says, 'sure,' and he jumps in on this story about the most honest man he's ever met.

And he tells me about how when he was a kid he always tried to do the right thing: went to church, got good grades, minded his elders. He was a good kid. And he got a lot of attention for being good- people were nice to him. It felt good to be good. So it became his focus and goal in life to always be good. And he was- he was always good. But then he tells me how after a while, the older he got, the harder it was for him to be good, because it got harder for him to know what good is. There were lots of voices around all telling him how to be good, and all telling him something different. So he tells me about how he decides that instead of being good- which is very confusing- rather than that, he's going to be honest instead. Honesty is the heart of purity, which is the highest good, after all. And besides, it's easy to be honest. All you have to do is tell the truth. All this he's telling me.

So then next he says about how he starts to be the most honest man he's able. And he goes around being honest about everything- always telling everyone about how everything really is. And he becomes a very honest man. Then he says about how after he starts being honest, he loses all his friends. And about how that's to be expected, because no one really wants the truth about anything, anyhow. So then he goes about trying to make some new friends, but he has to be real careful and explain everything real good when he's telling people the truth so they'll understand better and not have their feelings hurt too bad about how things are. And this goes alright for him for a while, but eventually he decides that being honest is just too much work. He's always having to explain everything too much so people won't take it too hard when he tells them what's what. So he decides that being honest isn't the thing, either.

Then after seeing how the goodness confused him and the honesty exhausted him, he decides that instead of doing what he's supposed to do, he's going to set himself to start doing those things he wants to do- call his own shots on good and bad, right and wrong- you know? And that seemed like a pretty good idea to him, he says, and it worked for a while.

But then this is where he stops his story. He's on his knees, picking weeds off the lawn, and he looks up at me with those sad eyes, and you know what he says, Tommy? He says, 'But that didn't work, neither. I guess there's just no clean way to do it.' And he says it about as forlorn as a man can say a thing. 'No clean way to do what?' I ask him. 'To be righteous, Brother, to be righteous,' he says and then he puts his head back down and keeps picking weeds. And that's the last thing he says to me about anything.

At this, Mr. Milo pauses as if waiting for me to speak, and looks me unwaveringly in the eye, still with that mischievous glint. "And?" I say, after a few too many seconds of awkward silence. "And what?" he says back with mock ignorance, a self-amused smile growing on his lips. "And what? Well to start with, what happened to Ricky? And, who is this honest man he met? And what's the whole point of the story? Let's start there," I answered with animation.

"Well," said Mr. Milo calmly, after sucking air through his teeth and thinking on my questions for a second, "I guess maybe he never did meet an honest man. Maybe that was his point- there are no honest men. Or maybe Ricky was the honest man, that could be too. Or maybe it could be that he did meet an honest man, but never got around to telling that part of the story. I guess I really don't know, and he didn't say. Now, as for what happened to Old Ricky, I do know a dash more about that... I didn't see him on weed duty for about the week after our conversation, so I started asking around a little to see what the skinny was. Word had it his sentence had come in, so off he went- I never saw him again." Then Mr. Milo gazed off over my shoulder, his mind maybe on some detail or memory of Ricky. "What was his sentence?" I inquired of my friend after a moment of shared reflection. "Hmm?" Mr. Milo responded absent-mindedly, still with one foot in his reverie. "What was his punishment?" I repeated. "Oh. Capital. Hanging, I think, or maybe firing squad- I forget." "What! Wait, why?" "Oh yeah, well, I guess the guy killed his whole family. Butchered them with a garden rake when they wouldn't stop interrupting his show. Gruesome. Total psychopath that Ricky, as it turns out... But you know, there's an important lesson here: *It doesn't do you any good to be too good."* "I'm not sure that's the lesson of this story, Mr. Milo," I said uncertainly. "Well, you know, it's one of them at least," he replied airily, then beckoned to Mojo for another drink.

I must have looked unconvinced because then Mr. Milo slaps me on the back with what felt like the flat side of a ham and five bananas, but was actually just his open palm, then he says to me, "You gotta take your good advice when you can get it, Tommy. Don't overthink the source!" And with that a deep rich laugh rolled from him.

I was considering this nugget of barroom wisdom when by happenstance I glanced across my watchface and noticed the late hour. It was a solid 90 minutes past suppertime. With a start, I told Mr. Milo I'd best be shoving off- my eats was fixin' to be ready. I tidied the tab and bid farewell to my rapscallion friend, then headed back out to the van and took the long way home. I wasn't too harried about being late. My Rebecca knows better than to give me grief when I've been out walking it off. Trust me, she knows.

****

against a blaze of starlight

It's tough to be seen against a blaze of starlight, especially when you're not the star yourself. When you're just a backlit mote, you're barely seen at all. But there are advantages to flying low, and one of them is that no one thinks to worry about where you're going or what you're up to. Not when you have a famous sister for everyone to worry about.

-Meh. Not grabby.
-What do you mean?
-That's kind of a limp start. And yet, it's also weirdly erratic. What's all this with the sister?
-She's famous.
-Yes, I gathered that much. But famous for what?
-I don't know; I haven't gotten that far yet. Actress? Maybe a famous television star. She's a television star.
-I'd say put a pin in this one. At least rethink that start... Now come on, let's talk about something else. You pick the topic.
-Actually, there has been something on my mind lately.
-Great; what is it?
-Well, I'm not sure it's something I should bring up with you. It feels kind of sacrilegious.
-Don't you worry, sacrilegious is my specialty. No thought too big. Please continue, I insist.
-It's this notion of 'conjuring' that I keep bumping into. The idea of being able to summon energy and matter. To manifest things into existence. I keep thinking I'm doing it. Could that be? Is it real?
-What do you mean 'is it real?' Do you mean 'does it conform to logic?' If so, then not logic as you know it, no. Or do you really mean to ask, 'is it possible?' Because if so, then the answer is, 'yes.' Here are some things to think about as you muddle through this one: force yourself to stop thinking about it as *energy* and *matter*: two separate things.

Think of it instead as *energymatter*: one thing, because that's more like it. Also, have you ever been to a place that gave off a distinct mood; a place that had a "vibe," good or bad, and then something good or bad came of it? Some event occurred there? That's an energymatter. So you already get the concept. You already know that energy and matter can be influenced, so quit acting like the concept of 'conjuring' is such a mindblower. And once you're able to start thinking about it as one thing, try not to be conscious of energymatter. Try not to conjure it. Try instead to simply acknowledge when something you've put to the universe comes to pass. Assume a state of 'unintentional awareness.' A nuanced instruction, for sure, and it's harder to do than it sounds. There's more to it than that, but this will get you started.

-'Unintentional awareness,' got it. I'll meditate on this. But I have to say, it seems a little rearward-facing, since you only acknowledge a thing you've summoned after you summon it. Not much power in looking backwards. Know what I mean?

-Well, the more you practice the meditation of 'unintentional awareness,' the clearer your energymatter signal or beacon- for lack of better terminology- will be. Which is also to say, the clearer you will be sending and receiving energymatter signals. And the stronger your energymatter signals, the more you will be able to conjure. That's one very rudimentary way of thinking about it. Like I said, there's more to it. But that's all for now. So off you go.

****

two men in the car of a train, one sleeping

I am sitting in the car of a very fast train, heading across a very wide space, on a very long journey. Across from me sits a man. He is sleeping. Given the rose and violet hues of his hooded robe, I'd say he's from Tokyo, though he's maybe from as far west as Nagoya. I'm not used to the air here. It's springtime and there's weird pollen about; my nose doesn't like it. I sneeze loudly and the man sleeping across from me awakens.

"I'm sorry for disturbing your rest," I say to him, "I'm not used to the air here- it makes me sneeze." "That's quite alright- in fact, thank you for shaking me loose," the man replies. "You wished to be woken, then? Were you having a sleep terror?" I ask him, "I have plenty of those." "No, not at all," the man answers me, "in fact, quite the opposite. I was in a dream with my children and my wife. Our dog was there, too. We were together in the mountains," says the man. "That sounds like a beautiful dream. Why would you wish to wake from such a dream?" I ask him. "Because it was more than a mere dream; it was a memory, too. The memory of a time meaning loss for my family; a time of deep sorrow for those whom I love most. To recall it makes me melancholy. But I am grateful to have these dreams, all the same. They are the golden-jeweled treasures of my soul."

As we speak the train slows gently, stopping to silent rest. The man rises to go. "This is my station," he says tersely, then departs. With a cool swish of doors I am left to myself in the train car, and return to thinking.

****

suppering with a friend

I am in the dining car of a train, suppering with a friend and discussing travel. He has just returned from the continent. There are two empty wine bottles on the table before us. Beyond the window's reflection of this scene, we rocket silently beneath the canyon's rim and across the desert floor. The night's full moon casts silver spells upon this empty land. My friend is quite drunk. I only drink water, and in the mornings black coffee.

"Unfortunately, the whole thing soured me on Brussels," my friend is saying, "which is a shame, because I'm told it does have charm. If you know where to look." "It really is too bad- the effect the narrow-minded can have on a chap," I say in agreement, "one bad encounter and you're put off on a place." "They tell me the city has charm, but I didn't see it, not at all," he talks still. "You gotta know where to look they say. I should have never gone into that place. But a guy doesn't know a place- not when he doesn't know the place- you know? Now Amsterdam, there's a place I love," continues my friend. "Singularly abstract," I agree robustly.

His attention is grabbed and he looks over my shoulder. "Say, isn't that Ashley just arrived? I haven't seen her in a minute. Who's that she's with? My god, she's still a treat." I turn and see her and she sees me. The warmth between us crackles like a campfire. "That's her fiancé, Michael," I reply. "Lucky bugger," he says, "she's still a treat." My friend and I stand as Ashley and Michael arrive at our table.

"Hello, Darling," she says and kisses my cheek, lingering imperceptibly. Her once-knowing hand rests lightly upon my shoulder. My hand rises to her shoulder too and I kiss her low on the cheek- near the edge of her lips. "Hello, Love," I say back. Everyone greets and we sit. The waiter brings more wine.

Ashley and Michael are traveling to Spain to see the bulls, Michael tells us. From there, they'll return to the front range, where they live and are quite happy, he tells us more. They're to marry this New Year's Eve. "In Courchevel," Michael says. "Great skiing," my friend replies. "Congratulations," I say to all of it.

The 2-minute arrival chime for Gibraltar Station bongs pleasantly, and my friend and I wish Ashley and Michael safe travels. They are leaving the train and transferring to the Paris Line, heading north for Pamplona. My friend and I will stay aboard and bend south, toward Marrakesh and beyond. "Good-bye, my Darling," Ashley says with a kind smile and moist eyes. She kisses my cheek once more. "Good-bye, my Love," I say softly back, and embrace her gently for just a whisper too long.

Gibraltar Station comes and goes and I bid my friend good night. I head to my sleeping car and ready myself for bed, hoping to rush asleep. It's only in my dreams where I can see her now, you see.

****

we make no sound

I am on a train speeding across a savannah, but we make no sound; this mag-rail is silent as a serpent. I am leaning against the glass of the observation car and smoking, much to the porter's chagrin. For reasons I don't understand, I feel surly. The porter- sensing his station- knows he should take some sort of action against me, but he doesn't want to. Abandoning his worry, he decides to ignore me instead and wanders off the observation car and away. I finish my task, tap my bowl, then return to the pullman to review the daily wires.

I sit in the day car with the news and my mood remains off. Horrible things are somberly reported to me by the Gleefully Glum: someone is cheating someone somewhere, war brews everywhere, parts of a missing stepmom have washed ashore. Et cetera. As I sit reading in impotent indignation, a woman enters the compartment and sits down next to me, close. Her perfume- as ever- has some mystery to it. I can't see her face but I don't need to, I know her all the same. She is the Girl With No Name.

The train slides quietly along and we sit in comfortable silence. Our hands remember each other easily and twine gently into one. Our shoulders lean together, our heads tilt softly in. My breath slows, my worries dissolve. A few effortless moments pass between us and she speaks: "There you are," she says with a playful laugh, "I've been looking everywhere for you." I smile at the joy of having her near me again, though, remembering this isn't real, I quickly sober. "Of course it's real," she says teasingly, having read my thoughts, "it's just that it hasn't happened yet."

(My mind averts toward some screaming buzzer... an alarm.) And I'm awake.

****

madison

And it had been a late night before, because R and I had put the kids to bed, then gone out front to share a joint and talk about things *for real* this time with no filter and no yelling or any of the other dramatics we usually do when we talk about the hard part of ending it- but not killing it- and what that's going to look like when we're ready, which we're not. And it was one of those perfect Montana nights that's so clear you think you're looking down through to the pebbled bed of a glacial creek and not up and into the cloudless infinity of a billion glittering, slashing, quicksilver stars. And all of it- the looking up past the pine tips to the snow globe sky, the train's hollow whistle wailing to us from across the lake, the forest twigs cracked and cracking by animals you can't see- all of it made for the kind of gentle mountain vibe that lets you know everything is going to be ok in the end.

Next morning I woke refreshed, despite having rested off little more than a nap. I made coffee and started breakfast for the house. R's cousin Kevin was visiting from Nevada with two of his daughters and a neighbor kid. Kevin spent six years in the army as a forward observer doing dangerous things. He'd been hurt but not badly, and he'd lost friends to war. We talked about the military and high school wrestling and public works construction and lion hunting and bear guns and cooking with fire and things like that. Kevin was possessed of that quiet confidence reserved for folks who know they can survive in the wilderness. I liked him immensely.

"Pronghorn antelope," Kevin was saying. I'd asked him his favorite game to eat. "Nine out of ten guys won't agree with me, but that's because they don't dress them right. It's all in how you handle the meat." Antelope have hollow hairs filled with an insulating oil, he told me. If the brittle hairs break, the oil spills onto the meat and sours it.

When Kevin skins an antelope, he begins between the horns, slicing back along the spine to the tail. Then he peels the skin away from the spine and down around the belly, folding the hair in on itself like a jellyroll as he goes. Next he butchers the animal, handing chunks of it off to his kids, who run them back to the truck, wiping the meat down with white vinegar and throwing everything into the cooler. "My goal is always 30 minutes from kill to ice," he says. "Do it right and you'll never have a better steak," he assured me, and I believe him.

I'm running a bit behind, but it's no matter; the schedule is loose. I throw my gear in a bag and load the truck. I'm missing a few pieces of kit, but spend little time worrying about it; I'll borrow what I'm missing and buy what I can't borrow. I bid the household goodbye then hit the road. It's six hours' drive from here. I pass out of the Flathead and down through the Swan Valley, taking the lakes to my right. The air is perfect and the sky is perfect and I roll down the windows and let the wind roar. I can't hear anything over the sound of the landscape passing me by and it's just how I want it. I untether my mind from its leash and it goes.

I think about my family and my girls and how I can help them become what they will. I think about work and deadlines and the money I need but don't have. I think about the ledge I've just stepped off of and how I'd better learn to fly before I hit the ground. And I think about the mess I'll make if I don't. And all of it is punctuated by moments of awe as I look around myself and take in the snowed peaks and the long green views and the fern floors and the high running waters tinged brown by the thaw and the rains and the gold-blossomed canola fields all along it all. I stop for black coffee at gas stations when I want, and there's not much traffic for the season, and I go as fast or as slow as I feel, and everything is just right.

About an hour past Butte I notice the truck ahead of me is starting to wobble. He's pulling an open trailer loaded down with what looks like everything he owns, and his control is slipping. He swerves a little and seems to get a handle, but then the trailer weaves more and its amplitude grows and things fall apart and it's bad. He swings hard to the right then overcompensates and swings hard to the left, losing control entirely and slamming into the median, blowing a tire, and knocking his truck around 180 degrees. The trailer jackknifes across both lanes of interstate and spews a household's worth of furniture, tools, boxes, and detritus across everything. The truck and trailer and all the stuff screech and tumble to rest, and it's a real mess.

There's one truck between me and the wreck and he and I both see it coming and we both slow down so that neither of us gets tangled up in it, too. We pull to the side of the road, hazards on, just before the wall of wreckage. No one is hurt, but the driver is spooked pretty good and so is his friend. A line of cars and trucks and big rigs begins to grow along the shoulder of the highway and without a word about two dozen travelers converge on the pile of destroyed memories and we start clearing the road to make room for traffic, just like Montana does. A state trooper arrives and steers everyone through the gap and then I get back in my truck and pass by the shocked and grateful faces of the nearly-dead and I drive away and keep heading south.

An hour or so later I enter the final valley and I grab one last cup and some gas in Ennis before making the final push to the rendezvous. I pull into the Slide and find our campsite and JT has just arrived too and we greet like brothers and then we set to make camp. Turns out the camper keys are back in Bozeman though so we cut out a screen with a box cutter and JT crawls through the window and opens the door and we get in the camper and set everything up and it all makes out just aces.

By now the sun has dipped beneath the western ridge, but there's still some light so we decide to rig a rod and throw a few before dinner. We take turns catching fish off the boat ramp while the other one smokes grass in a camp chair and offers encouragement. "What do you know about antelope?" I ask JT at one point. "Not much. I hear they smell like corn chips when you dress them," he replies. We talk about women and work and reading the waters and nymphs versus drys and the beauty of the place and about how many fish we're going to catch tomorrow.

There's a fraternal energy to the campground and JT introduces me to a number of his friends as we're making our way back. He knows nearly everyone here including all the guides and most of the campers. "This is John," he says, as I shake hands with the man before me. He's a clear-eyed, sturdy old trout slayer; probably somewhere in his 70's.

He and his friends are drinking beer and barbecuing next to a massive fifth-wheel. "John made me this rod," JT continues, holding up the 11 foot, 2 weight we'd just been fishing. "I love this rod," he says and John beams. We chat with John for a few minutes more about sourcing graphite blanks, then bid him good night and head back to camp. The wind blew through while we were gone making a bit of a mess, but we clean it up quick and light the grill and get the steaks on and eat t-bones and salad and drink boxed wine and share another smoke and have a dinner that's finer than anything served that night in any city anywhere.

I wake next morning from a dreamless sleep and we have coffee and a piece of cold chicken for breakfast, then I set to work for a few hours and JT does too. We meet up again at lunch and grill some burgers then get rigged and ready ourselves for the river. While we're prepping, an angry storm blows through so we don our foul weather gear and sit in the rain telling jokes and wait out the black squall that's heavy but blows through pretty quick. Then the sky clears and we head to the river's edge and wet wade down the bank.

For the first mile things are slim and we don't even get a take, but we keep moving down and while we do another storm comes over the ridge and turns right toward us and this one is nasty. We find ourselves stuck in open country and there's lots of lightning and nowhere to go, so we lay our rods down in the grass and we lay down next to them making ourselves as flat as we can and we watch the river rush past us as the lightning and thunder rip and rage above us. Two ospreys fight over a nest in the distance and we watch that too. Once everything passes on we get back up and keep wading down. The storms have cleared everyone out so we have the river to ourselves and the fish start eating and it just goes. I get a couple on but can't hold them and JT catches everything.

We keep fishing down until we hit the bridge then decide to keep going a little further until it gets to dusk, which is plenty late this time of year. JT hasn't stopped catching fish and I never started and we're having a hell of a good time but it's getting on to dark so we pull out and make our way up to the highway and walk the few miles along the road to camp. We get back and decide we aren't quite done yet and there's still a little sky glow so we head over to the boat ramp and keep going.

It's getting real dark now and I can't see a thing and the bats are diving at our flies like crazy and it's all starting to get pretty funny, so I tidy up my rig and watch JT who can't see a thing either but it doesn't stop him a bit and he just switches to feel and he lands a huge brown in the pitch black and I'm not kidding when I say he caught that fish completely blind. There was no doubt before but there's less than none now that the dude is a stick. Dinner is cold burgers and chicken and macaroni salad and a frozen candy bar and I'm telling you, it's all just perfect. Both of us are whipped and I stay up a small bit longer because I want to write a little and JT goes to bed and I'm not far behind. I see my grandpa in a dream that night and I can't remember what we talk about, but it's perfect too and I wake up feeling all peace and easy.

We eat pancakes and hamsteak upriver at a flyshop cafe that JT knows, then we head back to camp to get some work done. I decide to stay on until early afternoon and put down some ideas I have banging about and JT makes calls at the picnic pagoda. He's sticking around one more night to do an evening float with a couple guide buddies of his and he invites me to stay but I've gotta get back. We reconvene early afternoon to tidy up the camper and break down some rods and I stow my gear in the truck and move the extra ice into the cooler that's staying and then it's time to go.

Driving back up is no less magic and beauty than driving down but there's something missing when you're thinking about what just was instead of what's to come, so I'm not quite as energized this time but I'm still letting the wind howl and I'm still thinking on things and I'm still taking in all the colors and mountains and sky. It's a fast trip home and it feels like I'm driving downhill and not much happens though I do split a patch of whitetails along Salmon Lake but none of them dash out in front so it's no harm no foul and I just keep flying.

I get home past dark and half the house is asleep, but the girls are still awake and they're glad to see me and I'm real glad to see them too. I unpack the truck and have a bite to eat and then take my first shower in three days, and it all makes me notice how just tired and relaxed and truly happy I truly am. And as I fall to sleep that night my mind drifts through the woods and along the rivers and it wanders past my final waking thought that life here is like living in the painting of a perfect and impossible place. And then I really am asleep and the dreams I dream are of all the waters I haven't fished and of all the fish I haven't caught. Not yet.

****

one angle of an abstraction

Think of it like this: we are all characters in one of God's dreams. (say it again) You are a character in one of God's infinite dreams.

Dreams have no boundaries- real dreams, sleep-at-night dreams never do. And we are similarly unbound. But we are also fleeting, because all dreams and their characters eventually end. Time is not infinite to us, not even in dreams. But for now- for right now- you are an unfettered dream character. Whatever your circumstances, this is where your character picks up in God's dream.

And dream characters live by dreaming rules- which is to say that there are no rules in dreams. Dreams rule themselves. And as dreams rule themselves, so do you rule this one. This one dream that you are in. This one dream of all God's infinite dreams that is about you. And your consciousness- that thing that gives us awareness and seems to have a voice- that is your direct channel into God's dreams: the energy source that absorbs all the voices of all the characters in all the dreams in all the ways and everywhere.

And the kind of character you are in this dream that is about you- what you do and what story you tell to God in God's dream- is up to you. And your story is told to God through your endless stream of conscious thoughts, that can only be controlled by you and that is the only thing you can control. Your lifevoice to God.

You are one of God's infinitely singular story tellers. What story do you tell God? What parable that is your life do you tell God so that God might add to God's golden treasure of divine wisdom?

And this is why you exist, why you are: to tell God a beautiful dream.

****

it doesn't work like that

-What are you going to do? You're running out of options.
-I *am* running out of options. I guess I'll be a writer. It's the only thing left, and honestly, it's the top of my list.
-Ok, so be a writer. Write something. Tell me a story.
-It doesn't work like that.
-It doesn't? How else would it work? Come on, tell me a story.
-Just like that, tell you a story?
-Yep. Anything. Anything can be a story, if you know how to tell a story.
-That seems forced. I want to write something that doesn't sound forced. The Greats never sound forced. I want to be a Great. Just writing something to have words on paper- that's forced. I want it to be inspired.
-So force something out, then massage it until it sounds inspired. Try that. You gotta start somewhere, so start anywhere. Here, I'll help. Write one sentence that sounds cool but means nothing. Now go.
-Alright fine, I'll play. How's this: "The world looks different from your back- looking up- bleeding on the ground."
-Not bad. Now take 'The' off the front and add two more sentences. Go.
-"On your back, gazing up from the ground, the world looks different. On your back, gazing up and bleeding, the world feels different. On your back, gazing up and bleeding- and hearing screams all around you, screams meant for you and your situation- you realize the world will never be the same, ever again." How's that?
-Ok, this is sounding ok. Let's change gears; now describe this situation in two sentences from the perspective of a bystander- third person. Go.
-"Girlfriend, groceries, wife, milk, boss, girlfriend, weekend, sex, girlfriend, dish soap: Terrance's mind was ajumble with the flotsam of his day, when the panicked shouts of those around shook him loose and

alerted him to the waxing chaos, just ahead. A crowd was gathering around the immobile form of a blond, mustachioed man who was on his back and bleeding; and doing very little else."

-Everything's fine. That's all great. Just fine. Now let's approach from a different vantage. Quick- without thinking- name an animal.

-Dog.

-Different animal.

-Fish.

-Different animal.

-Dog.

-You already said 'dog.'

-I like dogs.

-Ok fine, dog. Now tell me something about this dog- its name, distinguishing features, mannerisms, whatever. Go.

-Well, Dave- that's the dog's name, Dave- is maybe the most magnificent creature alive. His barks sound like moany screams because he can't hear himself talk, because he's stone deaf. He's got the underbite of a camel, and only one eye. The other one got chewed out in a dog fight. Though not a handsome, a very charming fellow, this Dave. Oh, and he's adopted. Well, more specifically, he was dug out of a dumpster in Mexico City and taken home by Anna and Mark, who now live in Montana, with Dave.

-So these kind folks found a deaf, half-blind dog moaning in a dumpster in a foreign country, and they took mercy on the animal and brought Dave home with them and made him part of their family? That's a sweet story.

-No, not... not exactly. You see, all that stuff happened to Dave *after* Mark and Anna got him. The dog fight, the deafening, the missing eye, the what have you.

-You mean...?

-Yeah, Dave was a perfectly healthy dog before he was ripped out of that dumpster (or, "dog buffet" as it's called in stray terminology) and forced into domestic servitude in a far away land. Getting "adopted" in Mexico is the worst thing that ever happened to that poor son of a bitch.

-Ok, let's just... let's stop here for a second and regroup. What were we talking about again?

-Well, I was just starting in on Dave for you: the most interesting dog in the world.

-No, before that?

-Oh; you were going to show me how to write a story.
-Ah yes. So I was.

****

the end

Sean Gallagher was born and raised in Phoenix. He studied English at the U.S. Naval Academy, and philosophy at Arizona State University. He lives in Montana.

Made in the USA
Middletown, DE
05 April 2024